Quarterlife

Quarterlife

Brent Stephen Smith

This is a work of fiction. All names, characters, places, and incidents are a product of the author's imagination. Any resemblance to real events or persons, living or dead, is entirely coincidental.

Brent Stephen Smith
brentstephensmith@gmail.com
brentstephensmith.wordpress.com

One

I give up. I quit. No more. Not one bit more. I will admit defeat and let my ego take the blows. It's okay, alright? It's okay. I'm not quitting anything major or walking away from something that could have ever been great. I'm admitting it has all been done before. Everything.

I used to imagine myself in a great big white room, staring at the possibility of painting words across the whiteness, filling in something new, and having limitless possibility. You reach a certain point in life when you realise it has already been done. The whiteness that covers the walls is not there due to absence, but abundance. Every possible thing of all shapes and colours already exists. I'm not the first one to note this. Of course, not. I'm also not the first to declare that because everything has already been done all we can do is try and do it better or differently. I'm not so clever. I have heard that in movies. I have seen that in television. I have read that in books. A professor at graduate school told me that about what was required for our academic research. It had to be original. In that case original meant doing something better or differently. Newness is something we all would aspire to, but it does not just appear. For all our aching as a society about forgetting the past, we never seem to forget the content of the past. Music gets repeated. Words get repeated. Some of the great minds in art and science were also the biggest thieves, sometimes knowingly.

I'm not here to steal. I'm not here to pilfer turns of phrase or bon mots from the great authors that came before. I would be lying, however, if I tried to tell you my ideas were new, that the thoughts behind them were created in a vacuum. That would be disingenuous and I think you would know better. Instead, I will stick to the great instruction: write what you know. Even if it has been done before.

So, let us start with the basics. An introduction is usually needed get the audience to buy in that this is their heroic protagonist.

Sitting at the computer desk, hunched over with poor posture, and typing in awkward form is Jonathan Jones. He's twenty-five years old, has poor eyesight and is beginning to bald. He's the kind of self-deprecating man that can joke about his flaws in order to win over the comfort of strangers.

-Hello.

You probably all know men like Jonathan Jones. As I have mentioned, nothing is new, everything has been done. Jonathan would describe himself as being a pretty good-looking guy. Varying degrees of handsomeness have been used by women he's dated to describe him. He has heard gorgeous and a few other words, but he likes to remember gorgeous. He would never describe himself that way. That would be vain. Jonathan is not a narcissist. He is a novelist. There is a huge difference.

Jonathan is typing feverishly away at his laptop, attempting to write a comedy. His first novel was a drama, which he heard a few good words about. However, most of those good words were about the few comedic bits.

-Give the people what they want.

Jonathan likes to mutter away at nothing. Don't be offended, readers. He is not a misanthrope. I wouldn't do that to you. It would be rude. He is just a frustrated writer who has not made any money with his writing. It's what the rest of the world like to call waiters, students, bankers, accountants, landscapers, bartenders, analysts, mechanics, doctors, and, of course, professional writers. These are people who just have stories to tell and want you to pay to hear them. You wouldn't pay to listen to your friend's vacation stories, but why not read their travel novel? Absolutely brilliant.

He was not writing a travel novel, though he had travelled a bit. Jonathan had no advice on where to eat in Marrakech or Madrid.

-You will find that fast food remarkably tastes the same everywhere.

Indeed. No, Jonathan was trying to write a comedy about the wild crazy adventures that university students find themselves in. It was really original. Seriously, he believed that at the start. Yes, I know. We all have flaws. At the very least, we can admire that Jonathan's flaw was ambitious.

In an attempt to make this task easier on himself, and following the instruction to write what you know, Jonathan had decided to draw on his own experiences and the experiences of his close friends. He had some concern about what they might think to read their stories in print, but this weighed less important to Jonathan than actually writing a novel. He is not a jerk. He is a novelist. There is a difference. In an effort to help avoid the embarrassment his friends might have when they read their stories in print, Jonathan was kind enough to use fake names.

-An alias is really all that separates non fiction from fiction.

Quiet, Jonathan. That is our secret. Invention is a beautiful thing. We invent stories. Really, we do. Believe me. Just like the Mona Lisa was an invented face. Da Vinci did not need any model to sit for him. Really.

Jonathan, for whatever your thoughts are, dear reader, thought to himself that he had at the very least a code to respect the anonymity of his friends.

In the introduction to his book he included a short passage to assure his readers.

I will not name names and I will not confirm or deny the actuality of the following events. Some are real, some imagined. Some misremembered, some mistold. I will just say there is a truth buried in these pages. It's the story of our youth.

The chewed nails of his fingers click clacked the keyboard, creating tone-deaf music for the eyes. Jonathan enjoyed the look of his words as they began to sprawl across the screen. There is something amazing and powerful about creating life.

~~It's also fun to destroy words with the click of a mouse.~~

Agreed. But, one must always remember that with the power to create comes the responsibility to create wisely. We have numerous examples: gunpowder, the atomic bomb, Milli Vanilli. Jonathan typed away, bringing life to his creation. He began to introduce thinly veiled versions of people he knew.

Nick was a tall, broad shouldered Nova Scotian, with a great appetite for beer and poor taste in fashion.

Nick was not named Nick, but everyone who knew both Jonathan and Nick would almost immediately realise who Jonathan wrote about. If they did not then, they would when the story progressed, even if the story was real, imagined, misremembered, or mistold. That was the trouble with writing fiction. Whenever you write about something real, it becomes hard to mask. Likewise, whenever something that is actually pure invention is written, everyone assumes it happened. No, I can assure you, with almost certainty, Ursula Le Guin has never lived on an anarchistic utopian moon colony.

John le Carré actually did have some sort of spy career with MI5 and MI6, but was allowed and encouraged to write by his boss, on the condition he use a pseudonym. I have to say that I have seen several spy movies and rarely does the protagonist have the time to hunker down in front of a typewriter for months on end, working on his "masterpiece", without some baddie trying to kill him. The fact that le Carré was allowed to leave MI6 with his writing success tells us two things: he probably wasn't the second coming of James Bond as a spy and they really wouldn't miss him, or, he is still secretly one of the deadliest spies in the world, cunningly doubling as an elderly best selling author of spy novels ("The Perfect Cover" – raves the *New York Times*). Either way, he was probably a difficult and moody guy to have working for you ("Are we done yet with this interrogation? I have got to get home and type my daily 2,000. Also, do you mind if I write about this? Screw it; I will do it, anyways. I'm John le Carré.").

Jonathan is not John le Carré. There is nothing exciting about his day job to write about. He has one of those non descript bureaucratic jobs that spies in John le Carré novels get to use as a cover for their adventures ("I'm sorry, honey, I have got to go to a sudden conference in Akron, Ohio. I will be back on Sunday. Please ignore the bullet wound in my shoulder.") – but it's actually his job. There is nothing in his daily life that he considers worthy of putting to paper. Sure, there are the occasionally interesting interactions with his friends and co-workers, but they are hardly anecdotal, more descriptions of banal events. They would bore you at a cocktail party, let alone placed in the only book you brought on vacation.

It was wild, when, by mistake, I got sent an email by mistake. They wanted Julie Jones! And, I'm all like, I'm Jonathan Jones. Oh, I tell you, we had a great big laugh about that one, then and there. True story, I kid you not.

So, like all men of a certain age (any), Jonathan is filled with nostalgic thoughts of a bygone era when things were better and he wants to write about them. I should clarify that; these are nostalgic thoughts of a bygone era when things were remembered better and it's that misremembering that Jonathan will write. It was a horrible habit that Jonathan has developed, though he comes by it honestly. I would argue that a large number of people like to think that there was a time when things were better. It should come as no surprise when the world is filled with people like that. American conservatives cannot agree at what exact point America was better ("Who wants to say British rule? Put your hands down!"), but they will throw out confusing and anachronistic references to the infallible Constitution, the Second Amendment, small government, and Reagan, trying to weave them in to the belief that they all coexisted simultaneously. At least with the Amish, they are very precise as to when time found its Goldilocks era ("Not too many bright colours, nor too few horse buggies"). They believe things were just fine up until electricity. That is where they draw the line. We can all agree that the Amish aren't destructive jerks about modern progress. Luckily, for both the Luddites and us, history has left them in the past. Now those guys were jerks. Can I get applause from all the exploitative Dickensian industrialists? You guys know what is up.

Like Chuck Dickens and the social inequity of the Industrial Revolution, Jonathan was inspired to write about his own formative experiences. It just happened to rest in his mind as being positive ("Come on Dickens, I know you keep mentioning the slums, but have you seen these ridiculously cheap pantaloons we can now buy?"). That is what happens when dwelling in the minutiae of the present: we romanticise the minutiae of the past. So, Jonathan typed away, imagining a grand vision that all the exploits of his youth held eternal truth to the many men like himself that now found themselves dead at twenty-five.

Funeral for the Young

A novel by Jonathan Jones

He sat on the edge of the mattress, letting his back arch lazily forward. A few more hours of sleep would be welcome in his body; a few more hours that is all he felt he really needed. It was not an option. Leaning forward, further still, he saw the old hardwood floors beneath his feet. They were cold and they were soft. One hundred years of wear and tear had created deep grooves between the bed and the door. Lesser grooves led between the bed and the window. Jonathan smiled as he looked at the window. A brilliant whiteness beamed through the thin curtains. Mornings like this should be enjoyed, he thought. Sentiment began to knock thoughts in to his head. He couldn't help it; today was a day prone to sentiments and nostalgic memories. There were days before that he wished he had stayed in bed. Regrets find strange homes in the mind, always wedged between memories. They force themselves to be remembered, to always lurk behind ostensibly positive thoughts. There were mornings, beautiful mornings, when staying in bed provided the adventures the outside world could never afford to let him enjoy. For every day like that, there were a thousand that Jon got out of bed. He knew it, sitting up on the mattress, half committed to leaving, that today would add to the thousands. A cosmic abacus slid even more pieces towards that unfortunate tally as he stood up. Lifting up his towel and the jeans he had left on the rocking chair, Jon opened the door and walked down the corridor to use the common bathroom of the bed and breakfast.

Hot water pressed against his back and he woke up. The daze that lingered around his mind dissipated in the shower's steam. He loved this part of the day with a bittersweet affection. Every morning, half formed thoughts danced awkwardly around his brain. They became formed in full, as the heat of the shower hits. Sometimes those half thoughts were revealed to be brilliant ideas and they could excite and charge through the day. Other times, the sharpness of the thoughts in the shower revealed their folly. Jonathan did not like it when that happened. It was always better, in his mind, to dream. If dreams still held the promise of fulfilment, they were magic. To be ruined by imposed external realities was hardly fair. In Jon's mind reality did not have editorial power. Ideas were free to run their course and to discover their potential. The fantastic feeling of what if drove his mind. Everyday he could see a beautiful woman and let the mind wander - what if?

Dried off and dressed in denim jeans and t-shirt, Jon joined his family in the dining room. The owners of the bed and breakfast had made croissants and were serving them with cereal and fruit. Jonathan's father was eating a grapefruit, cut in half. The sight was so familiar Jon had to confirm with his eyes that they were indeed guests. His mother was engaged in a discussion with his grandparents about how good the homemade croissants were. The discussion was running to its close with the conclusion that they fell in between the categories of really good and really, really good. The owners expressed their gratitude for the compliments in the down to earth folksy way small town proprietors do. A kind of aw shucks reaction that seems genuine despite the fact that you know they hear this every day.

"Are you excited, Jon?"

"I guess, I don't know. It's just a ceremony."

"It's a pretty big deal. I don't think you realise that."

"Sure, I don't know."

"I can't remember the last one I went to. It might have been one of our nieces. We are just so proud of you Jonathan. Grandma is very proud of you. I hope you know that."

"Thanks."

"We all are."

"Thanks."

They were all proud; Jon knew that. Doubt sat in his mind, not due to a lack of support or pride from his family, but of his own thoughts. It always came back to that one big question that every man has asked throughout the ages: but what does it all mean? Or, to put it more bluntly: so what?

"Do you know how long the ceremony will be?"

"A couple hours, I think."

"Hopefully they will have air conditioning."

"It's in a gymnasium, I don't think they will be able to effectively air condition it with a thousand people jammed in there."

"They will likely have to open up the doors and windows."

"Won't that cancel out the effects of the air conditioning?"

"Yes, it would, but if they have one thousand people in a gym, it might be more effective to have the doors open and let a breeze in."

"Why wouldn't they have it outside?"

"Yes, why wouldn't they have it outside?"

"It's beautiful today."

"Today is beautiful."

"It's supposed to be absolutely beautiful this afternoon."

"Why wouldn't they have it outside when it's so beautiful?"

"It rained last year."

"Oh, it rained last year. That makes sense. We wouldn't want rain on a day like today."

"Rain on a day like today wouldn't be very enjoyable, I can tell you."

"It's a good thing they moved it inside this year, I would hate to be outside in the rain."

"To think of those poor parents and grandparents, forced to sit in the rain and the mud, for hours. I wouldn't like that."

"Oh, the mud, that would be awful."

"They were smart to put it inside this year. There will not be any mud inside. Nor rain, if it did happen."

"You don't think it will rain this year, do you?"

"It shouldn't. Today is supposed to be beautiful."

"Yes, certainly beautiful. Rain would ruin that. Oh, and all that mud, too."

"Good thing we will be inside."

"It's going to be hot inside that gym, though. It's going to be hard to keep it cool."

After agreeing that today would be beautiful, the gym would be hot, rain would be awful, and mud is generally a bad idea, Jon's family set a time for departure. The drive through the countryside was beautiful in June, something that Jon had never seen before. Every summer he had returned home to find work.

"It's beautiful."

"Today is just beautiful."

Every detail of beauty was on full display, as if Creation had spared no expense. It all seemed fleeting, though.

"You picked a pretty great place to go to university, Jon. It's gorgeous here."

"You should see it in February."

Cold thoughts of disappointment flurried through his head, knocking over all the warmth thrown at him in abundance that day. He felt like an inmate on death row, having a laundry list of things to do before he graduated and no opportunity to check them off. It would all be over so soon. He looked around the car of adults and grimaced with the thought that by this evening he would be one of them. Of all the courses he took, none could prepare him for that reality. There was a switch that would be flicked that afternoon that Jon wasn't certain he was ready for. Did anyone else feel that way?

They arrived at the university campus and were greeted with a smiling parking attendant who quickly told Jon's father, in English and French, that they were free to park in the lot next to the football stadium. Jon's grandfather giggled at the bilingualism.

"You don't hear that out West."

They walked in to the sports centre and followed the directions of the signs, and the people standing in front of the signs repeating what the signs said, to get to the gymnasium where the ceremony would be held. Jon made sure that his family all knew where to be and then left them to join the other graduates.

It felt unnatural to see his classmates in suits and dresses. Four years of becoming familiar had created an environment of casual acquaintanceship, where everyone knew everyone, or at the very least felt as though they could know anyone. Who were all these suits, though? They were unapproachable robots sent to replace the young vibrant students Jonathan had known.

"Hey Jon. Are you excited?"

"Oh, hey Jerry, I guess, I don't know. It's time to leave, right?"

"Yeah, for sure. I think we've seen too much of some of these professors. It was getting awkward running in to them at the SAQ."

"I don't know what's more embarrassing, them seeing you or you seeing them?"

"Probably the frequency that we were seeing each other there."

"This town can do that."

"Yeah, I think my liver might appreciate me moving on."

"It's been good, though."

"It really has. If I didn't feel so old I would stick around for a victory lap."

"It hasn't been that good."

For every milestone they had experienced that had chiselled them in to what they were, it had also left scars.

"So, what's next, Jerry?"

"I got a job."

"Just going to become another jobber."

"Yeah, it looks that way."

"Right on."

They stood and laughed awkwardly about some of their favourite moments in class. Jerry had spent the majority of his degree taking the same courses and that familiarity left Jon with melancholy. Was Jerry feeling the same doubts? He had no idea about the rest of these suits, but was it possible Jerry also felt like he was being led to the gallows?

Jonathan looked around for other familiar faces. For one reason or another he knew he wouldn't see his former roommates. Charlie and Drew had one more year left, Gio was off on basic training with the military and due to splitting the graduating class in to two ceremonies, the person he wanted to see most, Nick, was scheduled for a different time. With the exception of Jerry, Jon felt like he was going to experience this alone. For the ceremony seating, they arranged the graduates in a line alphabetically by surname and then Jerry was gone, too. Surrounded by the husks of people he once knew, Jon was alone. Welcome to the real world.

The line of convocating students were led around the back of the sports centre and told to wait. In their gowns, caps and hoods they echoed the academic traditions of medieval Europe. Jon could only think of the plague. It festered in his mind and took over his imagination. Instead of scholarly rites and the colleges of Oxford, he saw the dark mounds of corpses lining the narrow streets of London town. Barrows being pushed door to door to gather the deceased and to inform the diseased when the next trip round would be. His professors stood off to the side, wearing the finest regalia, befitting for the solemn occasion. He thought of the hangman and wondered what they drank to calm their nerves before performing an execution. He wanted to ask Jerry what some of their professors' favourite tipples were, but he was too far away. Jon imagined something like sherry or brandy in the old dead men's hands when they wanted to pause for reflection. Even morbid subjects like mortality deserved some thought. For the reluctant hangmen he imagined a harsh, quick drink of rum or rye, anything to give a spirited response to numb the mind. These were the ones who would lead the youth down the path to death. They didn't have the benefit of the hangman's cloak, anonymity during the gruesome action, but ensemble, as they marched in unison ahead of the students procession, they blurred together until it didn't matter. Like the unknown hangman, they might have executed the damned, but it was society as a whole who condemned them and came to watch the spectacle. All were responsible.

Jon obediently walked in the line, letting his eyes focus only on the hood resting on the back of the person in front of him. At this point he had forgotten even their gender, let alone their name. The cohort of graduates entered the gymnasium to the rapturous applause of the crowd. Jon was sure that nervous smiles crossed the faces of all his classmates, but he knew not what kind of nervousness. There likely were many who were excited for the next stage in their lives to come, beginning today. Jon wondered how many others might be nervous like him that this was the end and not the beginning. For every student that thought the crowds cheered for their accomplishment, was there another who felt that the crowds cheered as Romans feeding those upstart Christians to the lions? Was his generation here to be slaughtered for sport? In Jon's mind, there was a sneaking suspicion that their irreverence was to be punished. After opening their minds during the past four years it was unfair to close them up again.

There was a knowingness about the way his parents and grandparents spoke about life that Jon never wanted to be in on. Threats that he would one day get it and understand, he always hoped to be baseless and empty. Their exasperated faces sought an unknowing acknowledgement from him at the time. They wanted to be understood. Why? Why would they want to bring upon that pain in to his life? Was this the moment that it would become clear? Jon wanted ignorant bliss, but that cursed reality reared its head. It wouldn't go away.

The principal or chancellor stood up to the lectern. Jon could never tell one from the other. You find that old dead men look the same after time. All the distinguishing features tend to rot away in to the soil. Whichever skeleton it was began with a solemn speech, hidden beneath empty platitudes. He said meaningless words about the uniqueness of this crowd, about all their future accomplishments to come. He never mentioned the assembly line. Jonathan had a hard time understanding the entranced look upon the faces of everyone around him. Did they really hear meaning in the ramblings of a ghost inviting them to join him for tea in his grave? It was mad, why would we all consent to this? When was the waiver form signed? Jonathan worried that he had missed the fine print one too many times. Or was it every time? He hadn't paid special attention as the text scrolled across the bottom of his television. Did every commercial, whether for erectile dysfunction or automobiles, subtly place a disclaimer that at the most inopportune and unexpected time his independence would be lost? He was a part of the machine now and it was dust and cobweb covered, creaking its way to extinction. Was he the only one noticing this?

After the chancellor's ghost finished its speech, it invited to the stage another ghoul. The second old dead man was feted with a degree that carried the same honours as a mercenary's paycheque. For the next thirty minutes the imprisoned audience was subject to the tangential advice of someone of supposedly great accomplishments. Public speaking, apparently, was not among them. Jonathan couldn't focus at all on the words of the bought man. More empty platitudes spewed from his gob. Regardless of the intent, there was nothing inspirational about repetitious clichés. The graduates would have been better served by a proper eulogy.

"Looking around, I can tell you I see a lot of excited faces. They should be excited; we are told this is the first day of the rest of our lives. It's an entirely optimistic sounding phrase that they throw out at us to fill our cups with hope on a sticky humid summer day when we are all almost certain to succumb to heatstroke or gas. Gas, oh what a time to have it! Mentally I think it's at the back of most people's minds: don't pass wind on the stage. Today is supposed to be a mistake free day. Hear your name. Walk across the stage. Shake the hands. Miniature wave to friends and family. Walk off the stage. Walk down the aisle. Sit down. Shut up. All without passing gas. Or having your name mispronounced. Or tripping on a step. Or having a sweaty palm. Or a beet red face. Or waving in the wrong direction as you obliviously walk past all your friends and family, with the camera rolling and not a single chance for a second shot. This is the only take we get. I used to think these moments were supposed to be special, almost religious rites, but now after having been to a few I can tell you that they are just community theatre of the lowest calibre. The acting is wooden, the script worse. I have never seen one thousand people more relieved to go home at the end of a Gilbert and

Sullivan production by accountants. I don't know who to blame for adding all the pomp and circumstance, but it certainly does not help when they actually play Pomp and Circumstance at the ceremony. Between that and the medieval gowns, caps and capes I think we find ourselves taking this far more serious than it ought to. The beginning of the rest of our lives. Scary thought, no? Whatever they want to call today: graduation, convocation, commencement, firing squad, it does not matter. The result, I think you will find is the same. Today is not only the beginning of the rest of our lives; it's the end of what came first. Our youth is being sent to the slaughterhouse today and it's high time we accept it. The world will change around us today without any real choice. Like Dylan Thomas I want to rage against the dying of the light, but times are hard and I need to move on. I can't afford another semester of tuition. Besides, nobody wants to be that creepy old guy sticking around for the most ironically titled term ever, the Victory Lap. And with those thoughts, whether it's fear of being awkwardly on the outside looking in, or sticking around being the awkward insider far too long at the party, youth just passes you by. So why not go out with a bang? Fine, if only it were so easy. Most of these celebrations are actually affirmation for parents and grandparents to attend and see that their progeny haven't entirely messed up the past four years away. Let them attend, I suppose. They deserve a front row seat as we become them. Don't deny it. It only takes one handshake and a piece of paper and you, sir, have become an adult. It will no longer seem right to ever, under most circumstances, purchase alcohol in bulk again. But we never did that, did we? Give us a nice wink then.

No, we will never really get the chance to celebrate an end to hi-jinks and possible misdemeanours. It's all really anti-climactic. Working backwards, we get our final hurrah today in June and it's actually already too late. This is a wake. We haven't seen each other for six weeks, when exams ended and we all skipped town. And even those last few weeks were not really as exciting as we had hoped. It's hard to have wild, unencumbered antics when at the back of your mind you know you still have to write four papers, five exams and when you get a chance, you need to tidy up the apartment, including possible renovations, in order to get back your deposit. No, it all becomes a bit half hearted. And then it's June, and we stand around today asking those stupid questions; when did it all happen? My how time flies when you are having fun. What a stupid phrase that one is. Time does not fly faster when you are having fun. You get to immerse yourself in it. You are drawn in to the moment and it's as if time has nearly stopped and it's perfect. That's the thing. Time becomes meaningless because you get to live in the moment and aren't stuck having to recollect the whole damn time later. A night at the bar with friends could seem like months because of all the things we experienced. It's actually the opposite that they don't want to admit. Time flies when you are out in the real world. It churns along at the same pace in actuality, but they say the older you get the faster it seems to move along. It's all relative. According to a high school dropout, Albert Einstein, that means there is going to be less and less time for slow deliberation and reflection, kids. We are about to enter a world where things move at a steady clip and we just become passengers, like riding a conveyor belt to the grave. I had just begun to understand what it meant to be a conductor, finally in control of my life and I'm being told I'm just a passenger? That worry will pass the moment I realize that whether you are a passenger or a conductor, we are all sitting on a goddamned train the tracks decide where we go, and every little town we pass by is not worth getting off for.

There are a lot of nervous faces here, and I suppose it has more to do with looking down that track than it does worrying about whether they are going to pass gas on the stage. It's a perfectly reasonable feeling, I guess, nervousness. I'm terrified of my future. It will not matter whether I get to decide one thing or a thousand, the rules of the world are out there and all my decisions will have to be within them. How much autonomy will I get out of that? That worry will pass, too. The thing is that for four years we got a taste of something sweet. When we wanted to challenge ourselves mentally, there was always something. When we wanted to indulge ourselves physically, there was always someone. The only limits that we knew were word counts and if someone felt so inclined they could blow past a maximum count without any likely consequence. These are guidelines, man, guidelines. Fuelled by alcohol, drugs, sex, rock and roll, and philosophy, four years can be pretty amazing. And then, an end.

I will not get to give a commencement speech today. Don't be worried, it was not something given to me and then taken away due to some last minute antic of desperation or rebellion. I was never considered for the honour and I don't blame anyone for it. For all the exceptional things I have experienced, I'd never call myself exceptional and I have a lingering suspicion no one else would, either. I can't say that I would even enjoy it. I do, however, look around at all these nervously excited people and think they deserve a proper burial. Enough of my rambling, with this period of our life about to be officially culled, let me finally get to that eulogy.

Dearly beloved, wretched acquaintances, heartbroken ex lovers, indifferent administrators, bigoted professors, ignorant relatives, we are gathered here today to say goodbye to those we loved. They came in to this world, this beautifully flawed world, alone and they exit as one. At times like these numerous platitudes are often thrown out in to the air as if their meaning will fill hearts and minds with encouragement and affirmation. I promise you none of that. Our departed are not off to a better place. That I cannot say with any confidence. To be honest, some may go on to accomplish great things, others may wallow in mediocrity, which if I may add, is still slightly above what most deserve. A few will surely disappear in to obscurity, others will discover demons that pull them straight through the bottom and further down than imagined. Within this group today, lie some of the leaders of tomorrow, they will be responsible for making decisions that have a huge impact on the rest of us. Try to act surprised when you recognise them twenty years from now in the papers and on television. We all know which ones these will be. We knew it during frosh week and nothing has changed since. Say goodbye to ninety-nine percent of your favourite athletes. They were great, once, and now they will join the rest of the world. They might end up playing on intramural teams, or even some semi-serious adult leagues, but for the most part their athletic dreams are over. The other one percent will be seen on television warming the benches of our beloved national football league, you know, the one with eight teams. Congratulations to you, oh one percent, we are so very proud to see that the dream stays alive in you. We will make sure to mention that in the winter months when you come by to repair our furnace. I don't mean to be mean, but I must be realistic. When we are told we can accomplish anything, I believe it was said with an invisible asterisk. They never mentioned the fine print, but that's okay, when they do we usually ignore it, anyways. When you leave here today, your youth stays. You will return to a world you thought you knew, but will only become apparent to you now. Things are not as they always seem. Everything sweet has a darkness behind it. When you were really young you would be oblivious. As you came in to your own, here, you learned about the darkness and you rallied and signed petitions. You wrote papers that exposed the darkness and made decisions not to endorse it. When you leave here today you will continue to fight the darkness. For a while. You won't know it, but one day you will find that you are co-opted by things that you don't agree with. But it will be too late. Look at the nervous faces on everyone older than you here. They know it. But as much as you won't agree with it, as much as you will want to rage against it, the darkness pays your bills. You will have credit card debt, mortgages, groceries, insurance, and regularly occurring unexpected expenses that will make you compromise your beliefs. The frightening thing is that you are not alone. Take that with you. You are not alone. As much as everyone admires rebels, we are not forming a rebellion. Try to imagine your inner Holden Caulfield, take that thought and that spirit, and now try to imagine him middle-aged and working in middle management. Eventually it all dies out and we are all phonies. But hey, sorry, I didn't mean to put a damper on the party. Let's celebrate today the past and we will do it for the rest of our lives. We will have reunions and local chapter meetings. We will donate money to keep memories alive. They say you can't buy happiness, but I suspect many of you would like to differ. At the very least, you will try. For health, good cheer, and to remember our youth, I say we raise a toast.'"

Jonathan finished typing his first chapter and smiled admirably at the matte screen of his laptop. He felt as though he had accomplished something.

-This could be something really good.

The first chapter is possibly the easiest one to write. It starts out with promise. You have ideas running through your mind. There are notebooks lined with amazing phrases that had jumped out at you at the most random times: on the bus, in the shower, making love, whenever. With the first chapter you literally have carte blanche to use anything and everything at your disposal. Characters haven't been entirely defined and plot is something you worry about afterwards. It always feels good to get the first chapter out.

Two

After ending strong with the opening chapter, it's sometimes good to lead with something exciting to grab the reader's attention. Jonathan sits frustrated at his computer. He has several interesting stories from his past that he wants to put in his novel.

-How do I grab and keep their attention?

There are two ways I believe you can grab the reader's attention early on in a book. The first is to continue along a linear path. The reader has already invested time in the first chapter getting to know the character a little and has hopefully a bit of a piqued curiosity of where it might go next.

Jonathan is having a hard time trying to connect the next scene from the last. He had ended the first chapter with the imagined eulogy by the protagonist, an overtly cynical version of himself, sitting at his university graduation. It made sense that the next chapter should be that cynical character continuing and elaborating on his thoughts.

First Meetings

No one could hear a word of Jonathan's eulogy. Thoughts danced through his mind as he continued to sit through the funeral masquerading as a university graduation. It was refreshing to Jon how honest he could be when no one hears him. He imagined that was the origin of speaking behind someone's back. He didn't plan to speak behind anyone's back. It just happened in his head. He felt crushed watching his classmates all buried together with him, an ensemble macabre. He wanted time to roll backwards. There was still so much to do. There was so much they had done.

"When you arrive at university they take you to your residence hall and introduce you to the room where eighty percent of your best memories from that year are going to happen, and one hundred percent of your worst. They take you from checking in at the office and walk you down the path, asking illuminating questions about your hometown, what you plan to study, and if you will be on their team on trivia night. The correct answer to these questions are: random town, because you will forget it after meeting five hundred other new students this week and ask me again in a week; biochemistry, because that usually involves zero follow up questions; and yes, certainly. You will find that by trivia night they will have found other teammates and you are off the hook. After this wonderful introduction of useless, and possibly untrue, truths about yourself, the dutiful staff member walks you up the stairs of your residence hall and opens the door to your new home. Inside you will find four walls, a desk, a lamp, a chair, a window, and, of course, the bed. Try not to think of the bed before you arrived.

Seriously, don't let your mind think a single thought about it. It will drive you mad when you do. Don't think about the bed.

"So, would you say the room is in excellent, good, fair, or poor condition?"

"Sorry?"

"For the agreement, we need to ensure that when you move out, it will be in the same condition as the day you arrived."

What had the previous owner done to the room? Don't think about the bed!

"Oh, I don't know. I can't see anything wrong with it."

"You seem nice, and I don't want to make it difficult for you at the end of the year, so let's put it as in good condition."

She winks with that assuredness that tells you that every room on campus is really in excellent condition but she's doing you a solid. You are special. Don't think about the bed.

She leaves you to the room, where you start to unpack your bag in to the dresser and the closet. There is a stack of linen on the bed. Don't think about the bed. You make the bed, but try really hard not to think about it. This room, and specifically this bed, didn't exist until the moment that woman from the accommodations office walked you in. There is a magic machine that spontaneously creates accommodations from the moment a key enters a door. This building was built in 1965, but this room is brand new. Don't think about the bed.

And then, out of nowhere, you think about the bed. You are usually sitting on the bed at that moment. All that random assurance you had given yourself on your trip to university, that this would be when you are finally free to experience life, that this was the time to try new and exciting things. Every person who has lived in this room since 1965 has thought those very same thoughts. It's too late not to think about the bed. You start to wonder how often they replace mattresses. At this point, no answer will suffice. It could be every thirty, twenty, ten, or two years and you will not be happy. Once you get over those thoughts, usually when in the company of someone else, it gets easier.

It was at that moment of general uneasiness sitting on my new bed that I began to explore the accommodations. When I said that the room was four walls that was a bit of an understatement. There were, in fact, five walls. There was a half wall that separated the front of my room, the part with the door and front closet and the back half, where the desk, windows, and, yes, the bed, lived. In that front part of the room there was also a closet, a sink, and another door. This second door appeared to go in to the neighbouring room, like in a hotel. I examined the door, looking for any signs that it would open in to another dimension, possibly one with a fresh mattress. I noticed at about eye level there was a small, sliding security lock. It was barely longer than an inch and when it was engaged at work, as it presumably was then, it remained precariously unassured. I reached out and slid the lock back. Drawing as much air as possible in to my lungs I turned the doorknob and opened the other dimension door. Inside was not another world, or barely even another room. It was what was optimistically described as a bog. It was nothing more than a small square room with a toilet and a shower. Across from my opened door was an identical, closed, door. I took a step closer to see whether there might be that second dimension hidden behind. What was there was far more interesting, and frightening, than I could have imagined.

Gio opened his door to the bog and we were six inches apart in a tiny square washroom. A wild mane of dark brown hair covered his head. I didn't know it for sure, but my suspicions began, that this was the lanky illegitimate lovechild of Tommy Lee and Stevie Ray Vaughn, conceived in one frantic night of acid and blues based guitar jams.

"Yo."

"Hi, I'm Jonathan. I guess we're neighbours."

"Right on."

"Where you from?"

"Belgium."

Of course, I had moved across the country to attend some small university with the hope of meeting interesting people and fate would deliver me the Walloon offspring of Def Leppard and Hendrix. I suppose it couldn't get more interesting.

"Oh, that's cool. That's in Europe, right?"

Thank you memory for stepping up at that crucial moment. I knew where Belgium was. I was well aware that Brussels was its capital. I knew it had a king. I had learned that bastard dialects of French and Dutch were their national languages. All of those facts seemed to resist any relay from my brain to my mouth.

"Yeah."

"I'm from B.C."

"Oh, cool."

This was the first person I had met that honestly didn't care about a single detail of my existence. He didn't question me about what town I was from, whether I skied, what I was going to study, or if I would be on his trivia team. I knew I would like Gio.

"I think we're supposed to head outside at three for some sort of rez orientation."

"Alright."

And that really was it. Gio was just this Belgian enigma who disappeared behind the bog door until three. Muffled ZZ Top permeated our common wall.

I went in to the hallway and saw the other floormates moving in to their rooms. There were eight of us to the floor. Gio was in the corner on our side of the hallway. Then myself. Next to me was Midge, a modern languages student who despite her white small town upbringing was likely to study Ebonics as her major. She at least had Bob Marley on one wall and 50 Cent on another. Next to Midge was Whatsherface. Her name does not matter, and indeed none of them do as I'm handing out aliases, but hers especially didn't matter, as after years of knowing her none of us were ever entirely certain about the truth behind any of her statements. Rumours swirled that her dad was connected with the Russian mob. Or maybe he lived and worked in Saudi Arabia for some sheikh. Or was in prison somewhere in Quebec. It does not really matter, as I can't really say anything about her. If university is a time period built for making superficial human connections ours would be on the poster. How do you know someone for years and not actually know a thing? Across from Whatsherface was Nick. Nick was the first Nova Scotian I had ever met and I continue to use him as the benchmark for what good Maritimers should be. He was a tall guy, broad at that time, with a terrible fashion sense and a bawdy laugh. Every moment was his. You know the type? The type of person who could enter a room and own it, even when he just didn't care. When we gathered, Nick set the pace. Next to Nick was his bog mate, Mark. I don't really know how to describe Mark. He was the artistic, musical type. We once caught him coming back in to the residence at five in the morning and had assumed he was off with some girl. Mark assured us he had actually been playing his sax in the woods, as it felt like the right kind of night to do that. Next to Mark, and across from me, was Melissa. There was a constant haze around her, though you wouldn't guess it from when she moved in. What do you say about people raised conservative who discover themselves at college? I guess I'd include myself in that column. If you have an answer let me know. Melissa's bog mate was Sally, a flighty acting major who spoke with great "brahvahdoh". You'd never guess that she and Nick came from the same planet, let alone province."'

As Jonathan sat there, drinking unhealthy amounts of coffee, he read his second chapter and thought it was okay. Not great, but okay.

-Shit.

These were hardly inspiring words of confidence from the writer, just two chapters in to his own novel. That's the beautiful thing about writers; they are all manic depressives. Maybe not all writers, though certainly a large number of them. They are the first to fly to the heavens at a whiff of their own genius and the first to come crashing down, not just to earth, but right through its crust, at the first instance of failure. They really are an excitable bunch.

Jonathan's miserable despair at his words lashed at him viciously. What a fool he was. How could he have believed that his words had any value?

He was going to lose any reader's interest with a pedestrian recollection of his youth.

This happened. Then another thing happened. After that, a third thing happened.

This is when Jonathan thought of the second way to grab the reader's attention early. It's a bit of a gambit, but when it works, it really works. You shock them.

Jonathan decided to set aside "First Meetings" for later and took a stab at the shock gambit.

On Duty

The lieutenant couldn't believe his eyes. These men, these heroes, were men. And they wanted to see ladies. It had to be tonight. Of all the nights for him to be on sober duty. Sure, why not, he thought, when he was scheduled. He never really enjoyed the mess hall dinners. Sure, he got drunk. Everyone did. But there was not some form of lingering need within his bowels to be at those dinners. If anything, the dinners were just a start to the evening. The dinners were the appetizers. These young men could create any sort of havoc on their own afterwards and that was what made these nights special. Or what the lieutenant thought was special. After tonight the bar was to be raised by men who had won a war. This was not the same as a bunch of part timers, those weekenders, with their cushy university lives going out carousing on a Thursday night. These were men. These men had needs, and damn you if you get in their way.

Gio floored the Mercedes down the highway, periodically gazing at the backseat through his rear view mirror. Not his, this was Tommy's car, a beautiful boat of a 1980s Mercedes Benz, the kind of car lesser African dictators would own. Tommy was squeezed in the back seat, as he was quite a large man himself, with two Second World War veterans, neither of whom was looking all that frail for their age, or their state. On top of the three men lay a stripper; still in her kit; with a fur coat worn over like a blanket for good measure, it was February. The bottle of Jack was being passed between the four of them as Tommy giggled and the war vets laughed riotously. The stripper didn't seem to give a damn about humour and every fourth pass of the bottle went down without ceremony. Barely keeping Gio company in the front seat was a second stripper who alternated between lying back, letting her head rest between the seat and the door, and hunching over the front console, snorting lines of cocaine. Every attempt by Gio to grab her attention was met with indifference or over exuberance. The bitch just wouldn't converse.

The car drove around the night swept city prowling for any sort of action the kids could show the vets. It was hopeless. Gio was beginning to fatigue. He was surprised by the stamina of the two vets, who surely had to be at least eighty years old. The silent, morose stripper in the back had been persuaded to give a "private" dance for one of the

25

old men, while the other watched. Tommy alternated between sneaking a look and curling over to the side with glee. The girl in the front had passed out, with her head diagonally resting between the seat and the door. Gio kept looking over and tried to admire her naked legs. This close, and at this hour, with sober eyes, she really was not so beautiful. It was a wonder she could make enough money to support her coke habit. How many generous generals must she know? But this was not the time to reflect as Tommy began to bark in the back.

"Gio! They want to see my guns."

"What?"

"They want me to show them my collection of guns."

"Are you nuts, Tommy? You are pretty wasted."

"Come on, Gio. We will go to my house and pick up a gun or two."

At that point one of the old guys joined the conversation.

"Lieutenant, I want a gun in my hand."

"I'm sorry, sir, but I really can't let you do that, now."

It was five in the morning and Gio was chauffeuring three drunken soldiers and two coked out strippers to no particular end in sight. He didn't want to pick that end.

"Fine, forget it."

Tommy looked disappointed. His fat, stupid face had really got its hopes up to show the old men his collection, his pride. He would have even taken them out in to a field and let them shoot at targets, maybe the JD bottle on the floor of the car, whatever they wanted. He just wanted their admiration. Growing up, he wanted nothing more than to serve his country.

Gio just wanted to go home. It was one thing to take them out for a few drinks, but things had got out of hand. How did this all start? He was sober, but tired. If he tried he could piece together some version of what happened that led to that moment. They had been at the mess hall for their dinner on a Thursday night. Gio was on duty. That night, several veterans visited the reservists. Two of them took a shining to Tommy. Tommy invited them out for drinks after the mess hall. The drinks took place at the strip club. The uniforms, and the money flowing from them, caught the attention of two strippers. The club closed at three. Tommy, the two veterans, the two strippers and Gio all piled in to the car and drove around town. The story was a jumble. Where did the Jack come from? Was it the mess hall? Did Tommy have it before? Was that really how it happened? Gio hadn't seen everything. There was a period where he was socializing with other reservists at the hall. Did they come to the club too? What happened to the other veterans? Gio could have sworn he saw at least four or five of them go in to the 'rippers. When did the commanding officer leave? He was at the club; Gio knew that.

This had been a test of patience for Gio as he tried to be the same devil may care person he was when he was drunk. But he was not drunk, and he did, somehow, care. Consoling him through the night had been two packs of cigarettes. A limp one hung from his lips as he and Tommy dropped their guests off at the hotel.

Gio got to bed at six. He pulled the blanket over his head and disappeared. The whole night flew through his mind, a thousand times, each one slightly different than the first. He didn't know what direction was up or down. He just closed his eyes.

Jonathan liked that bit. He thought he was back on track with his book. Nothing was a better story about how far off they had gone as young men at university. It was one of his favourite stories from the real Gio. It was dangerous and absurd.

He didn't know where to put the next part, so he just wrote it down and put it to the side for now.

"Later that morning, after four, maybe five hours sleep; Gio stumbled out of his room and greeted us with a grin.

"You will never believe what happened last night."

I don't. But a part of me wants to buy the mythology. A part of me wants to believe that anything is possible when Gio is there. He rarely seemed to be the catalyst for anything, but everything happened to him in those days. As for today, I look around at the crowd of awkwardly smiling faces and don't see his. He is supposed to be at basic training right now, but I'm never sure with Gio. His mom had wanted him to come to the convocation ceremony; I know that. Maybe she has the same lingering doubts about everything he says. Maybe she needs to physically see him walk across a stage to believe that he had spent four years enrolled in study. Come to think of it, I have the same doubt and I lived with Gio for four years."

Somehow, somewhere in the book he'd let that cynical eulogist connect the dots. Linear progression is for squares.

Three

Jonathan sits at his workstation with the sulk of a lost puppy. After a productive weekend of writing he had to return to work. John le Carré had the benefit of having a cool job before his writing took off. Jonathan Jones was disinterestedly working with a spreadsheet. It certainly was not a spreadsheet of how many Soviet spies' necks he had snapped on the weekend. It was a basic table of some statistics his boss had requested for the afternoon. Jonathan sips his coffee.

-Hey, Jon. Have you gone for a coffee break, yet?

-Yeah, Michel. I'm actually just working on it right now.

The paper cup rested in his hand, providing the obvious clue.

-Do you want to go for a walk, anyways?

-Sure.

There was only so much disinterested boredom a man can take at one time. For Jonathan that limit was about twenty-seven minutes.

-How was your weekend, Michel?

-It was okay.

-Did you get up to anything interesting?

-No, not really.

-Oh. Did you see the game on Saturday?

-Yes, I watched that.

-I thought it was pretty good.

-Yes, not the best I have seen, but they played well.

-They look pretty good.

-They should be in the playoffs this year.

-You think?

-If they play as well as they can, then yes.

-If they play as well as they did Saturday?

-Better. They need to play better than they did on Saturday.

-Yeah, probably. It's a weak conference, so anything is possible.

-That's true. But, even if they get in playing like they did on Saturday, if they play like that in the playoffs they will not last too long.

-Definitely. I totally agree.

-Did Philippe come by and talk to you?

-No.

-He thinks that they will win it all this year.

-What game was he watching?

-He claims the same one.

-Hometown fans.

-Hometown fans.

-It's always the same.

-Always.

-Always.

-What did you do this weekend, Jonathan?

-Oh, I wrote a little bit.

-Oh yeah, are you starting a new book?

-Yes.

Michel had been one of the few people that had read Jonathan's first book.

-What's it about?

-I want to write something fun, a comedy about the university experience.

-Oh.

-Yeah, it will be different than the last book.

-How so?

-I want to fill it with far more action. There is the possibility for a lot of crazy things to happen.

-Yes, that's university.

-Exactly. Everyone can relate.

-Regrettably.

-I thought you didn't believe in regrets, Michel.

-No, I don't. I just couldn't think of the word for it in English what I meant.

-Oh, okay.

They stop at the coffee shop while Michel fills his reusable mug. Jonathan felt like a dick while he drank from his paper cup. He had three reusable ones sitting at his workstation.

-Did you see if there were any good movies playing this week?

-No, I haven't checked.

-It's been a while.

-It has. We should get a group to go.

-Yeah, maybe.

-So, tell me more about your book.

-It's basically a version of myself telling a stream of consciousness style story of all the amazing, life affirming things that happened to my friends and me during university, while trying to draw the connection that life after university is the beginning of the end. I use the metaphor of death a lot in the book.

-That's a good one.

-You agree?

-Yeah, I really don't feel too much excitement about all of this.

-It's not what I was anticipating when I was a kid, or even a teenager.

-No, of course not. Everybody wants to grow up and be something cool and amazing and be with cool and amazing people. Instead I get to go for coffees with you, Jonathan.

-Thanks buddy, the feeling is mutual.

-It's perfectly natural to be disappointed. We should all be disappointed.

-It seemed like all of this was supposed to be somehow better than it is.

-Yes, that's exactly it. They told us when we were young it would be better than this, and it's not and they knew that.

-You mean it's always been underwhelming?

-Absolutely. Just look around and see we're living in a culture of mediocrity.

-Yeah, that's just it.

-What's the last big innovation that you can admit changed your life?

-Computers, I would think.

-No, not really. We were born in to that generation. Computers are scary and amazing things to our parents and grandparents. They're like sliced bread to us. So ordinary.

-Remember when they changed the way they cut foot long sandwiches? I do. That was revolutionary. From the v cut to the straight slice. I can still remember that.

-That's mediocre.

-No, it made sense; you can now fit more veggies in to the sandwich.

-Do you hear yourself speak sometimes, Jon?

-I do. I still think that was a seminal moment in our youth. I will talk to my kids about it the way my parents talk to me about the introduction of the metric system.

-The metric system.

-Yep.

-Another reason to hate Trudeau.

-Hey, let's leave Pierre out of this. He wouldn't have gotten the idea if it hadn't have been for the French Revolution several hundred years earlier.

-Alright, another reason to hate Robespierre.

-And he got what he deserved.

-That's right, the guillotine was probably calibrated in metric, too.

They returned to their office and parted ways at Jonathan's workstation. Jonathan looks at his watch. It reads ten thirty nine, or about three units of disinterested boredom until lunch. He sits and reads the news on the internet. He drinks more coffee. He sighs. Jonathan Jones is a modern man.

-Hi Jonathan, do you have a minute?

It's Jonathan's boss, dropping by to check in. Jonathan had several minutes to spare.

-Sure, how's it going?

-It's going pretty good, you?

-Good, thanks.

-I see your duster is coming in pretty good.

-Thanks.

Jonathan had been growing a mustache for a charitable cause. It was something he had actually forgotten was growing on his face.

-I have actually seen a lot of guys doing that this year.

-Yeah, there is a bunch now. It seems like a pretty popular idea.

-Think it will bring back the mustache?

He laughed. They always laughed. Jonathan wondered why. It was just facial hair and it grew naturally on the faces of men. It would of course come back in to fashion. These things always did. But the fact that it was being grown temporarily, almost ironically, for charity made it notable. That was the extent of a challenge that they were willing to undertake. So long as they shaved when it was all over.

-I don't know. It seems to be out of fashion right now.

-A lot of beards, though.

-Yeah.

Hipsters had brought back the classic beard. It was the perfectly lazy accessory for an underachieving tribe. Hipsters are just old ass teenagers, Jonathan thought. He also thought he wanted to be one. He loved the music they listened to. The debates they got in to. The freedom they had to drink terrible beer without any shame. Instead, he found himself sitting in a cubicle with his boss talking about spreadsheets.

-So, you think you will have those numbers today?

-Yeah, probably just after lunch.

-Great, thanks Jonathan.

This is what it had come to, thought Jonathan. Thousands of years of human progress had led to this moment. He was going to be able to give his boss a spreadsheet of statistical numbers sometime, probably after lunch. I'm sure Kant would be proud.

It was hardly a triumphant moment, but then again, nothing was particularly triumphant in this era. The model had been thrust forward in the 1950s and for all the pretending that society liked to do that things had changed, it had remained particularly stagnant ever since. To be sure, some things have come, Jonathan thought, but they were mere reforms, tweaks of the system, and not complete game changers. This was the great era of moderation, set forth by the nuclear family, and held steady ever since. People can argue all they like about the dissolution of nuclear family in recent years, and they can cite divorce and teen pregnancy rates to support their cause. They might also want to ask why gays are so strident to get the same rights that married heterosexual couples have. Even if their sexual orientation is different, the social norms, the very fabric that supposedly holds this whole mess together is still what they want.

-They can have my cubicle, too.

Remember when I told you that Jonathan likes to mutter things? He was at it again. It was a soul depriving existence, Jonathan found himself in. He didn't hate his job. That would be far too harsh. He liked it. He liked what he did. He liked his co-workers. He liked the money. But in sum, he didn't love it. And really, if we're honest with ourselves, is that not what we've been told to go reaching for? All those years that our parents and grandparents, teachers and coaches, role models on all fronts kept reinforcing the thought that we could live our dreams.

-This is not my dream job.

No, it likely was not a career that Jonathan had dreamt of as a young boy. There was not a small LEGO cubicle he played with. He had wanted to be something beyond that. To be fair, that's what all boys wanted to be. They really had no reason not to. Idealism and optimism are horrible ideas that plant themselves in the heads of children and don't leave until horrible realities replace them, often at that moment what we might later describe as a loss of innocence. Innocent? Jonathan questioned the whole concept. Naïve. It was all bullshit. Did parents actually believe what they said? When do they stop? Is this like Santa Claus? Enough deception, please. Jonathan felt like screaming at the top of his lungs that this was the end. Instead he sat quietly at his workstation, click clacking at his keyboard, click clicking with his mouse, compliantly doing what he was reasonably paid to do. It really was hard for him to make a fuss when it seemed like everyone else was in on the racket. Was this the Truman Show? Would it all come crashing down when the set starts to fall apart or his best friend forgets his lines? That was the dream. Not an idealised place in the distance that everyone hoped to reach. No, the dream was this charade that everyone agreed was real. It's okay guys, Jonathan thought, I won't mind stopping now if you do, too. That would be fantastic, if it were true. Jonathan was just beginning to realise that there was no stage production surrounding his life. It was real. And real, much like reality television, was boring. The moment it becomes slightly more interesting more questions ought to appear.

So, instead, Jonathan started retreating back in to his own fantasies. Instead of thinking about the possible future, as his parents and mentors had always urged him to do, Jonathan thought of an idealised past. Why did everyone keep talking about future plans and places? Everything has already been done. There was nothing left to do. Anything he had wanted to do was just a mirage. There were no oases in the horizon. That was as sombre a thought as any young man should think. Futility for the next fifty to sixty years is hardly motivating. Neither was repetition and routine. Jonathan wanted to break free and he was disturbed by both the possibility that so did everyone else on the planet, and that none of them did. Marx had urged the workers of the world to unite and throw off their shackles. It was a great start, Jonathan had thought, until you learn that the next step was not to do what you love or to find yourself, it was to reclaim the means of production. Apparently factories would be better places if the workers had shares in the business. Wouldn't they all be happier if they travelled through South Asia or if they took pottery classes?

-Hey Jonathan, nice 'stache.

-Thanks, Philippe.

-Did you watch the game on Saturday?

-I did.

-What did you think?

-I thought they played okay.

-Okay? Please, I think they played better than okay.

-It's still early in the season, but I thought they made lots of mistakes that they were lucky didn't come back to hurt them in the game.

-Yeah, but they looked so good when they were not making mistakes.

-True, but everybody does. That's kind of the point.

-So, you don't think they are a good team?

-No, I think they are a good team, but it's still too early to say that they are a great team.

-Do you think they will make the playoffs?

-Yeah, I think they will probably make the playoffs. They have the talent on paper, they just need to correct those mistakes I mentioned.

-I think they look really good and this could be the year.

-Every year could be the year, right?

-Yes, of course, but having watched them play in the past month I think this might be the best team they've had in a long time.

-Hopefully they live up to those expectations.

-Yes, hopefully. I will be the first one to cheer if they do win it.

-I would be happy too, but let's not start planning the parade.

-Alright, are you going to watch the game tomorrow night?

-Not sure, I might have plans, but if I don't I will flip it on.

-Cool, well if you do, let me know what you think. I think it will be a very good game. They are on a streak.

-Okay.

-Have you gone for a coffee yet?

-I have, thanks, yes. It's getting too close to lunch anyways.

-Alright, well maybe we can go for one this afternoon and we can talk some more.

-Yeah, maybe.

Philippe left Jonathan to return to his spreadsheet. He didn't want to admit it, but there was something comforting about the cells on the screen. He really did like his job, but liking something was not the same as loving it. Would you marry someone you like? Sure, maybe, he supposed, there are probably lots of cases of people who married someone they liked. But the aim, as years of instruction had informed him, was to find the right person that you love. It was not getting any easier on that front for Jonathan, either.

At twenty five, he found himself wanting to, being ready to, settle down. Not settle, but to settle down. If only he could find that person that he loved. It was easy in his younger days to find tons of girls that he liked. He might have even found a few that he'd dare to say that he loved. But now, even finding women he liked was a chore. There was not an abundance showing up at his cubicle on a daily basis. Things had been easier at university. Everyone got what they wanted, even if they were absolutely drunk.

Four

Jonathan drinks a beer as he looks outside at the dusk light. He's sexually and professionally frustrated. I think he would prefer that I just say he is frustrated, but I thought that you deserve a richer explanation for what he writes next.

He checks his emails. He's received a couple messages from acquaintances.

1. Hey Jon, how are things going? Are you coming home for Christmas? It would be great to catch up.

2. Hi Jonathan, I don't know why but you popped in to my head. Just thought I would check in. What's new?

3. Jonny! It's been sooooo long! We neeeeed to do coffee sometime. What's new with you? Have you been writing much lately?

Each of those acquaintances is female. Jonathan finds each of them pretty attractive. The problems: distance, distance, and boyfriend. It was always the same. Even when he went back to his hometown for the holidays it was hard to arrange to meet up. Things fall through. Girls conveniently get boyfriends in early December. Whatever.

Jonathan also received some messages from an online dating site he has been trying.

1. Wow, you write? That's really cool. I'd like to read it sometime.

2. Who are your favourite authors? I saw that you like Kerouac, that's very cool.

3. Your favourite singer is Damien Rice? OMG, so is mine!

He was just as unpleased to see these messages. Online dating was a drag, man. Jonathan found just as many flaws in trying to date the women he didn't know as the ones he already did. The problems: no photo (presumed fat), fat, and made up by me. Sorry, Jonathan.

-You are kind of an asshole, you know that?

I'm just trying to tell a story. You should be grateful I chose you. It's all been done before, so realistically I could have chosen to write about something more exciting like elves or spies. Instead I'm stuck with a worthless protagonist who sits around all day moping at work, only to come home and mope around there.

-Hey! I'm trying here. It's not easy.

No, it's not easy. But it's what you love, right? So do it. Write something.

-Just let me answer my emails first, okay. Let me have what little personal life I have.

Sure, no problem. I'm sure everything will work out on that front, too.

Jonathan wrote his goddamned emails. He then went to the fridge and grabbed another beer. He was frustrated, sexually and professionally, you remember? And frustrated people like to drink beer. They also like to smoke cigarettes.

-Please, no.

Why not, Jonathan?

-I have asthma. It's not a good scene, man.

Well, I'm just trying to build a good scene that adds an aura of stifled creation and having a little floating smoke in the air would look really cool.

-It's not cool. We're done with that.

I'm beginning to get a little frustrated, myself.

Jonathan slumped himself on his couch with a beer in hand and began to scratch away at a notebook. When he finished his beer, his second of the evening, he went to the fridge again. After beer number three he propped himself up, lengthwise on his sofa, with his knees up, his laptop resting against his legs. Then he began to write.

The Hunt

The clock struck four and the emptiness of the room was staggering. Gio crawled out from behind the futon and surveyed the landscape. In front of him were over one hundred bottles. They had feted Dionysus and Alexander Keith until they could bestow no further laurels upon their heads. The wreaths of the marathon had long wilted and Gio found Drew curled around the side of the upstairs toilet.

"You alright?"

"Yeah, I'm fine."

Drew was like a light switch. He would drink for hours, seemingly untouched by the effects of ethanol, constantly turned on. His voice never slurred beyond his normal country drawl. His eyes never reddened. He would be alert and engaged throughout the night. Spitting out folksy bon mots and axioms of wisdom like the seed of Twain, Drew would enrapture the attention of his courtiers. At some point in the night, long after everyone had endured enough punishment and called quits on their session, Drew would switch off and find himself wrapped around the toilet bowl, paying homage to the porcelain goddess. It seemed peculiar at first, to Nick and Jon, who were amazed at Drew's stamina, that it would be so sudden. Nick, of course, was one of the finest drinkers and had a respect for anyone who could keep up. Jon, however was perhaps the first in the evening to tap out of the proceedings. He was amazed that Drew always finished his night vomiting, while for himself it was only on notably excessive nights. He wondered if there was a particular point when Drew knew that it was too much and he ought to stop. Jon felt those moments and usually began to pace himself down. Sometimes the pressured encouragement of Gio or Nick would push him beyond that point and he would get sick, but it was never a surprise. Despite the frequency of his trips to the porcelain goddess, it always seemed to be a surprise to see Drew sick. He always seemed to be doing just fine, just a second ago. But as is often said, filthy habits die hard, and usually involve even dirtier replacements.

Nick, as far as any of them were aware, had never once vomited. If he had it was far more likely to be food poisoning, the result of his terrible cooking and not due to any amount of alcohol. They couldn't imagine how much it would take to shoot the elephant. This was a mammoth giant who had (mostly) survived the onslaught of seventy-four beers in a weekend. What would it take? It was the kind of stamina that was unmatched, with the obvious exception of Gio, who, as Jon fondly discovered, could vomit, leaving a mess for his generous roommate to clean up. Gio could also collapse at any moment, despite his seemingly immortal composition, there were the occasional bouts of humanity that brought to light how dangerous the volume of poisons he ingested could be. In his first semester of university, as he was impressing his friends with seemingly unstoppable waves of excitement and adventure, taking in constant streams of beer, bourbon and cigarettes, Gio built for himself a legend that even he could never live up to. Sure, there was his amazing day of drinking, where he bested a generation's record of inebriation, consuming forty-five beers in a fifteen-hour period. But that could never last. That pace of drinking was fine, though never recommended, it was fine for one day, or weekend. No human being could sustain that consumption over a prolonged period. His Icarian quest could only collapse. In sum, he spent over seven thousand dollars in that first four months at university, solely on alcohol and cigarettes, a tab that would make Blotto blush. Rather than stop or slow himself due to diminishing financial resources the only pause Gio could take was when, inevitably his body tapped out and forced him to lie in bed for a week at a time. It seemed that Gio in those days only had two modes. One was pure debauchery, the other convalescence. Both priests and psychiatrists would be confused. No matter the amount of pain he endured, the warnings his own body threw at him, begging for him to change, Gio could only return to his vices. When he joined the reserve forces Jon and Drew thought that would be the end of Gio's partying, but instead it fostered his ways in a culture of protected adolescence. All they wanted to do was fight, fuck and drink and Gio was game on all accounts. The only thing he lost was his unkempt facial hair, a spotty beard on its best days, and his long Messianic mane. He was a reformer, not a repenter. The dangerous thing about Gio was that others lost the visual cues he used to provide them with. With a small amount of effort Gio could join any situation in polite society. Once there, anything was possible. He was a silently ticking bomb of destruction. Nick was the triggerman.

Every group has a person that sets the tempo, that pushes them further down paths they ought not to go, seeking things they ought not to seek, trying things they were best never to know of. Nick was that man. He went where he wanted to go and never needed to ask for permission. He would do things without consultation and he would cause havoc. A tree or an old telephone pole might end up casualties when Nick was in a mirthful mood. That's what axes are for, after all. Nick was not stupid, in fact he was a genius, but an unsteady one, without limitations. His capacity for greatness in thought was only matched by his capacity for deep, dark thoughts. When he couldn't bring even himself to do something he thought of, he had a persuasive way of manipulating others in to fulfilling the deed. It could be little things, planting words of doubt in to other people's ears, or it could be larger, physically destructive things, Nick didn't need to hold the axe for the tree to fall. In Gio, Nick found his soul mate. Nick's mind had no limits, while Gio had no mind. He too could have intelligent thoughts, but they existed on a plane that none could truly interpret. It's hard to tell if someone is an idiot savant or just a plain idiot. He was, however a terrific listener and never once said the word no. If he hesitated, perhaps with a silent pause, Nick knew exactly how to push to get Gio to follow through.

"C'mon."

When Nick said that, it was impossible to resist. The women he had slept with knew it. The burning nostrils of his friends knew it, too. Somehow, Nick could persuade even the local police with a simple word. Jon was even subject to Nick's wiles, though he was nominally viewed within the group as the voice of reason. Nick could get Jon to do what no others could, and there was a bond between them that with a certain look Jon would welcome instruction from Nick. Nick respected Jon enough not to push him beyond what he knew Jon would truly be comfortable with. Jon drew a line for others, Nick pushed past that and created a second line for Jon. That zone between Jon's own line and the one created by Nick was filled with four years of moments that could only occur when Nick was around. No matter how wild Jon might get, if Nick wasn't there, he was able to straddle his self-imposed limit. Luckily when Nick was there and pressed him to go beyond, to seek a new reality and experience life on the outer frontiers, he always left Jon enough of a life vest so that he would never completely drown. With Gio, Nick had no limits. The two of them were going to fall as deep as fast as possible. Gio was a Petri dish and Nick the scientist. It was unclear whether Nick had read Jekyll and Hyde, but he fit that persona so well, although when he became Hyde he maintained his self-awareness. In Gio, he ensured that a night out with Hyde always included a doppelganger.

"Hey. I like your clothes. You look like you know how to wear them."

"What?"

"I said I like your shoes, baby doll. I like them. I want to eat them."

"Get away from me, freak!"

"That's cool. She just jealous."

"Yeah, man."

"So, Gio, you think we're gonna get her to fuck?"

"No. But it's probably a lost cause."

"Yeah, that's right."

"How about her, Nick?"

Across the bar they saw a cute blonde sitting alone.

"Time for daddy to strike."

"Give it a go."

The room twisted in front of him like a fun house. When he tried walking towards the blonde, Nick found himself going in the wrong direction, the floor tilting beneath his unsteady feet. A demonic shriek echoed behind him.

"Over here, Nick."

"Ah, Gio. There you are. I thought you had disappeared on me."

Nick thought he had said that. Instead Gio heard an incomprehensible babble.

"Angina. Theremin. Eye socket tube diapers, please."

"Nick, you need to speak in sentences."

"I know that. Where's the blonde?"

"Still across the bar."

"I'm going to go talk to her."

Nick traversed the distorted mirrors of the fun house and found himself leaning against the bar where the cute girl sat. He needed the bar to keep him from falling over. Somehow to the unaware observer, he just looked casual.

"Hey there."

"Hi."

"My name is Dick."

"Is it really?"

"No, that's just something I like to throw out there."

"Oh."

"Did you like it?"

"I can't say that I did."

"Alright, I will level with you. My name is Nick. Nick. It's easy to remember, because it rhymes with Dick."

"Thanks for the tip."

"You are a feisty one. I haven't even offered any."

"Whatever. I'm Julie."

"Right on, Julie. I like that name. It goes on your face."

"What?"

"I mean it suits you, Julie. You wouldn't make a good any other name. Maybe a Sarah or a Julie. You could be a Julie."

"I'm a Julie."

"Yeah, that suits you."

"Thanks?"

"No problem."

"So, Nick, what are you saying tonight?"

"I was just saying you look like your name could be Julie."

"What are you up to tonight?"

"I'm at a bar. What are you up to tonight, Julie?"

"Me, too."

"That's cool. Maybe we could be at a bar together."

"I think we're."

"Awesome. I'm glad you see me that way. I know we just met, but I think we've really made a connection."

"You are strange, Nick."

"No, I don't have a strange dick. What a weird question to ask."

"I'm sorry, it's really loud in here. I said you are strange."

"Whoa, Julie, easy, I'm not the one asking about dicks."

"You said your name was Dick."

"No, my name is Nick. It's easy to remember, though, because it rhymes with Dick."

"You've told me that."

"Do you want me to buy you a drink?"

"Sure, Nick. Gin and tonic."

"Gin and tonic? Gross. That stuff is awful. I mean how can you mix two terrible tasting things together and think that it tastes good?"

"I don't know, Nick, it just works for me."

"Awful, absolutely awful. It's like cyanide and turpentine with a hint of lime. I won't touch the stuff."

"I like it. In fact, I think I'm just about done mine."

"You should get another."

"I thought you were going to buy me one."

"Oh, no, that was just a general inquiry."

She burst out in laughter. In inexplicable terms, somehow this large goofy drunk had charmed her.

"I'm kidding, Julie. One G&T coming up."

"Thanks."

"So, what do you study?"

"Sociology."

"That sounds made up. Are you planning to find a husband here?"

"We're a bit early for that, Nick. How about we see about that drink first."

"Not a problem. The bartenders just pouring it now."

"I was not getting worried. What do you study?"

"Oh, I'm in bio chem, it's kind of like what you do, but real."

"You certainly have a way with words."

"If you think this is good, you should see me draw compounds."

"You chemistry guys are the biggest nerds."

"I don't think it's polite to call me fat, Julie."

"Haha, so funny, too."

"Here's your drink. I hope it burns your throat."

When needed to, Nick was able to rely solely on muscle memory, as the act of hitting on girls just became second nature, despite the fact he could barely stand or speak.

"So, Julie, what are the odds of me seeing your underwear tonight?"

"Haha, here, I will let you see right now."

Julie showed Nick the blue shoulder strap of her brassiere.

"Wicked."

"You guys are all the same, everything excites you."

"Not true. I don't find many things to be interesting at all, let alone exciting. It's pretty much just boobs at this point."

"Yeah, exactly the same."

"You get excited about boobs, too?"

"No!"

"I would think not. I mean every morning."

"It's still really loud in here, but when we're done our drinks do you want to pick up some food and chat. I don't know why, but I find you very interesting."

"Well, so long as we're going to make some bad decisions, we should be well fed."

A small smile ran across her face. Nick was oblivious, but it was a common smile in those days. It was the kind that girls had when they truly did like who they were talking to, even though they probably knew, at the back of their minds, this would never end up the way they wanted.

"Do you like souvlaki?"

"Like it? I love it."

"Really?"

"If I was not studying a real subject like chemistry, I'd probably go to donair school."

"Love it."

"Exactly. I'm glad you get that, Julie. Most people find it hard to believe that a wide shouldered young man knows anything about late night food."

She laughed again, drunk on both gin and Nick.

Jonathan sat pleased again with his work. There was always the ability to create unfathomable solutions when writing, and let them come to a happy close. Jonathan wouldn't write it then, it would take him a few more hours of drinking, but he would come back to this passage and add the rest; the truth part. Happy closes are for suckers.

She laughed again, drunk on both gin and Nick. There are some hangovers you can predict; this surely ought to be one.

Nick woke in a fluffy floral duvet, the kind of cheery sweet Swedish made linen that masked a despairing sadness at the roots. Was it Julie who was depressed or Nick? Were they both? That kind of desperate need for affection, the kind that drove thousands of young men and women to the bar looking for anyone to mate with was not unique to them, it just appeared across the board around drinking age. Why did they drink? Why did they consume that firewater? It placated fear temporarily, but created new demons to battle.

"Morning."

Julie's face was a mess. Nick was not sure whether it was his vision the night before, or the ravages of several hours of sleep and streaked makeup that made her appear far less attractive than he remembered. He knew he was no prize. He could barely walk the night before. It had taken a large effort to make his way across the bar to talk to the cute blonde girl. Where the hell was she? Julie was not a cute blonde this morning. Nick was not convinced she was even a blonde. With the bright morning light revealing much darker roots.

"Oh, morning."

"Did you sleep well?"

"Yeah, I think so."

"You tossed and turned a bit. It was funny you shook the bed."

"Oh, sorry."

"Don't apologise, Nick, you are good at shaking the bed."

She laughed an awkward self-created laugh. Nick lay still.

"Did you have a good time last night?"

"Yeah, definitely, I had a ton to drink and the music was pretty good last night. The DJ has good taste. I probably would have played most of those songs, too. I think I have almost all of them on my computer."

"No, silly, I meant with me."

Hesitation is the first admittance.

"Yeah, I did."

Nick couldn't remember anything between the moment he leaned against the bar to talk to a cute blonde and waking up in this Scandinavian garden with the natural brunette.

"Me, too. I really enjoyed talking to you last night."

"Oh, cool. Yeah, what was your favourite thing that I said?"

Nick needed clues at this point in order to leave this bed with some grace.

"You know. Those things you said. I don't know why, but maybe it was the way that you said them, but you definitely caught my attention. You are a very smooth operator."

"Yes, you could say that. What else would you say? Use specific examples."

"Do you not remember?"

"Oh, I do. I just want to hear you say them. I'd like to see if they have the same smoothness coming from a, from a, pretty girl."

"You were very naughty."

"I was?"

"Yes, I liked how you mentioned dick."

She grabbed him. Nick twitched. For all his surprise that morning at a disappointing conquest, Nick let her continue.

Did I mention that Jonathan was sexually frustrated? He joins a long line of writers.

"Do you like that, Dick?"

"My name is Nick."

"I know, but you told me it's easy to remember because it rhymes with Dick."

"That's true."

She played with him until he began to enjoy it.

"Morning sex?"

It was not ideal, but Nick had his segue to leave with grace.

"Yeah, but I gotta leave after. I have got to study for a midterm."

"Alright, just once, I won't keep you too long."

Four hours later a sheepish looking Nick walked in to his apartment. He was greeted by the knowing grins of his three roommates.

"Good morning, Nick."

"Hey."

"Gio says you picked up last night."

"Yeah. I did."

"Did you give her the jackhammer?"

"Did you take her for a wheelbarrow ride?"

"What did you do, Nick?"

"I ploughed her."

The roommates howled with laughter.

"Dude, Gio said she was a dog."

"Yeah man, she was hideous."

"You told me to go talk to her!"

"You could barely speak, I thought it would be funny."

"Well, have you had your laughs?"

"Yes. Oh, man, that was really funny."

"So, Nick, where did you wake up? Nice apartment? Somewhere on campus? Back to rez?"

"No, it was off campus. I don't know the name of the street. It was up the hill a bit. I was fucking lost when I walked outside."

Jon and Gio lost it. Drew maintaining composure asked follow up questions.

"How was the continental breakfast?"

"What?"

"Did you get toast, cereal, what?"

"She made pancakes."

"That's pretty impressive. A lot of effort there. More than most one night stands, I think."

"Yeah."

"You think she likes you?"

"Yeah."

"Do you like her?"

"No."

"But you stayed for pancakes. That's a significant moment in a blossoming relationship."

"Please, I don't want a relationship with this girl. I barely wanted to sleep with her."

"But you did."

"I know. Four times."

"No wonder you got pancakes."

"She was, how do I say this, very generous in what she would let me do."

"That's a plus, I suppose."

Gio joined in, having regained his composure.

"Yeah, but in the end it's a lot like riding a moped, isn't it?"

"What?"

"It's a lot of fun, but you wouldn't want to be caught in public with it."

All four of them broke out in laughter at the thought.

"I'm going to hell."

"Probably."

"This morning I thought I saw it when I woke up. It's pink and orange bedspreads and oddly shaped pillows."

"There is no need for that."

"I'm amazed those continue to exist."

"I wouldn't be surprised if each one of us has woken up in that situation. Not, of course, with the horrible moped that Nick went home with, but with others that had brightly coloured duvets and odd pillows made by guys named Jens and Carl."

"I hate those Swedes."

"The worst."

Jonathan didn't hate the Swedish. He knew quite a few of them. Lots of attractive blondes to get him worked up about without any hope of anything ever happening. That was the worst. Social networking had added to this problem by allowing those Swedish girls to post photos of vacations to Greece in their bikinis on the internet. At least with pornography we all know it's completely out of reach. It's way more frustrating when you actually know the person in the photo. There is always that faint thought that one day you might hook up.

No, Jonathan didn't hate the Swedish. He just wanted to use that line as a segue in to his next chapter.

Five

When I said earlier that Jonathan was not writing a travel novel, I really did mean it. He was not planning to write about hostels and hotels, food or attractions. He was just trying to put together a novel about his youth. All of his university experiences he thought carried value and weight. They helped define who Jonathan was, and he believed they helped define who he is. Part of that time involved travelling. Like so many young people he went to Europe.

The Night Train

Jon took the tickets from the agent at the counter and thought this couldn't be too bad. He had to ride a train for ten hours sitting upright. Spur of the moment things can sometimes surprise others, but Jon always felt there was an internal logic to foolish decisions. As was often said, it built character. He was not sure what kind of character he was building, but he found it to be entertaining at the time. When in need of killing two days while travelling by rail, but wanting to save on accommodations, it made terrific sense to ride two night trains. He would take one as far north as he could go, with a small layover, and then the other back south to Stockholm. In Stockholm he would meet up with his friends again. Some time alone was just what he needed after a few weeks of travelling with others. He hadn't minded it, too much. Sweden was basically just a hipster version of Canada, filled with skinny jeans and fey indie rock.

As he entered the car, Jon realised that ten hours sitting upright would be the least of his problems. In nearly every aisle, if not every seat, there were dogs and cats. Jenny, with a soft J, had fucked him over with her ticket selection. Jon was allergic to basically every animal on the planet.

"Hi, I think I'm sitting right there."

Jon let the man move his giant dog out of the way and stepped in to his seat. He could smell the dog, which was the first clue this was going to be horrible.

"My name is Jon, nice to meet you."

"Hello Yon, my name is Danny. You are Canadian?"

"Wow, yes, thanks. I'm amazed you recognised my accent. Most people assume I'm American. Very nice to meet you Danny, where are you from?"

"It's a very small town. You wouldn't have heard of it."

Jon felt insulted. He had always had a solid grasp of geography.

"No, no, go ahead. I'm pretty good with maps and so on."

"It's called Hagfors."

"Heck force?"

"Hagfors."

"I'm not sure I have heard of it."

"It's in Värmland, near Karlstad."

"Oh, I have heard of Karlstad."

"Right, so from Karlstad, you go north through Forshaga, then Munkfors, and then you are in Hagfors."

"Oh, okay."

"It's beautiful. You should really go."

"When would be the best time to visit? I will be leaving Sweden in a few days so I won't have time this trip. But, I want to come back."

"You must come in February for the Swedish Rally. They are very exciting races."

"Oh really? Are they the best drivers in Sweden?"

"The best in the world, Yon!"

"Oh, wow, I didn't know."

"Yes, it's too bad those damn Finns keep winning. We once owned them."

"Oh, in racing? The Swedes were better?"

"No, in real life. We used to own Finland, Sweden did."

"Oh, that's right, I think I knew that."

"They find one goddamned Mensa member who can drive a car and they think that they are all smarter than us. I don't think so. They have a hard time saying the letter H, too."

Jonathan felt a small petty smug sense of satisfaction inserting obscure references in to his writing that he knew his readers wouldn't get. I won't let him do that to you. Marcus Grönholm was one of the most dominant rally drivers of his time, and as Jonathan's bigoted friend Danny alludes to, Grönholm is also a member of Mensa.

Jon was trying to find the balance between encouraging Danny to speak about his country and avoid causing any further bigotry.

"Do any Swedish drivers do well?"

"Oh yes, Carlsson came third this year. It was the first time in five years that a Swede made the podium."

"Okay, do you think he could win it?"

"Yes, of course, I think Carlsson will probably win two or three Swedish Rallies before he is done."

Oh, Jonathan. You've done it again. You really are a sneaky bugger. Daniel Carlsson came third in 2006, five years after the last Swede to reach the podium. His driving career has been up and down ever since.

"Cool, well, if I ever come back, I will try to go to, go to Hagfors for the Rally."

"Exactly."

"And I want to cheer for Carlsson?"

"Yes, he is the best Swede."

"Alright, very cool."

"Where are you going on the train?"

"I'm going to Umeå."

"You will like it Yon, you will like it."

"Yes?"

"Oh, yes, it's very pretty."

"That's good to hear."

"Are you going camping, Yon?"

"No, I thought I would just take a train north for the heck of it."

"Is this American sarcasm?"

"No, no, no. I really did just have some time I needed to kill. I thought it would be fun."

"Oh, fun. Watch out for the Sami peoples."

Of all the overnight animal train cars Jon could have been forced to sit upright on for ten hours, he had to have been placed on the one next to Sweden's least subtle bigot. Danny's dog was not helping things at all either. Jon was not sure what was more irritating, Danny's words or the dog's dander. Jon's eyes were beginning to water, while his nose began to drip. He had been on the train for thirty minutes so far.

They lurched along at a lazy pace, as if no one on the train truly wanted to head north. It seemed like the conductor was giving everyone an opportunity to suggest that they go no further. Every second town became an elongated stop. There was more than enough time for new passengers to board and departing passengers to disembark and for the remaining passengers to sit impatiently. Danny explained to Jon that they did this to allow time for the pet owners to take their animals outside to relieve themselves. While Jon welcomed any opportunity for relief from the animals, he was still in terrible shape sitting up in his chair, with the air clogged with dog hairs and cat whiskers. He swore he saw canary feathers float by at one point. This, this was torture. He blamed Jenny, with the soft J, at the ticket counter for inflicting such pain on him. He was supposed to be a guest in this country. It was as if his hosts had decided at all pains to treat him as terrible as possible in order to ensure a short visit. Jon was well aware of the three-day rule. He had known for a long time that the optimal amount of time to visit someone for was no longer than three days, unless extenuating circumstances prevailed. In planning his visit to Sweden, Jon had planned for three stops, each of only two days. He had respected the rules, but it seems that Sweden as a whole was offended by his overstayed welcome. Jenny, with a soft J, had figured it out on his third day when he bought the tickets to Umeå. She knew then that he was going north and then he was coming back and spending a couple days in Stockholm. He was admitting his overstay in his plans to her. Surely Bjorn, Marcus, Elin, Jens, Nicklas, Elias, Emma, Lina, Patrik, Freddy, Andreas, Linda, and all the other Swedes in the line up behind him had overheard. What choice did Jenny, with a soft J, have, but to force him to realise he had begun to irritate the nation? She had to force him to sleep on the metaphorical pullout couch with the iron bar down the middle. Jenny, with a soft J, had to make him uncomfortable. She couldn't be rude. That's not what good hosts do. They can't be ill spoken of, so their hospitality has to be gracious and it has to seem genuinely welcome. But, Jenny, with a soft J, also had a responsibility to save her blonde haired, skinny jean wearing, hipster nation from an overbearing North American. Yes, by all accounts they would take his kroners, while they could, but if he wouldn't mind leaving in the near future they would all feel some relief. Relief was not forthcoming for Jon in the railcar. He was battling too many attacks at once on his system. One dog, at a friend's house, was a challenge, usually able to handle for a few hours, especially if combated with an allergy pill, but this was far too many. What was worse was that Jon had no allergy pills. Jenny, with a soft J, had forgot to mention this was the animal car. It was where they hid all the undesirable beasts from the other rail passengers. It was where they hid Jon.

Six

Thursdays in Jonathan's neighbourhood were relatively quiet. It was a residential area with a bit of park space in between the brick apartments and the townhouse rows. The people that lived in the neighbourhood came from all walks of life. There were young professionals like Jonathan, as well as Somali refugees, Quebecois retirees, university students and the occasional homeless person. It had a bit of a reputation for being a rougher part of the city, but that didn't seem to bother Jonathan, who liked to joke with his co workers that it just helped build up his street cred as a writer.

-Little Mogadishu is a fantastic place to live for that.

In reality he lived in what he affectionately described as a state of champagne squalor. His friends, like Michel, and he were living the lifestyles of young professionals, with LCD televisions, video game systems, leather couches, and original artwork on their walls. They drank imported beers and ate at restaurants whenever they felt like it. Their living was paycheque to paycheque, but they did it because they could. In reality they were all broke, but not broke like the homeless guys on the street. They could honestly tell the beggars they had no money on them, and then walk in to the liquor store and purchase six packs of their favourite Belgians. It was this lifestyle that was holding Jonathan back from fully embracing his writing as his way of life. Other people probably couldn't appreciate how hard it's to willingly walk away from a guaranteed salary with health and dental benefits and a comfortable pension. For all his wanting to, Jonathan couldn't fully commit to doing that. Not when his first book sold fewer copies than he gave away. For all the kind words he heard, kind words don't buy cases of imported beer.

That was the challenge for Jonathan. He sat at his workstation all day, comfortably doing work that he didn't mind, working with people he enjoyed, and getting paid a reasonable wage. What incentive was there to stop? When he wrote, it was a mad fervour of energy that would explode on his computer screen. He would love it at first; it might be the best thing he felt he has ever written at first glance. And then, Jonathan would be dismayed. It could be shit. It might be the worst thing that he has ever written. It might be the worst thing ever written in the history of Western civilization. He hated writing. It was frustrating. It was as frustrating as bad sex. Jonathan figured it was as frustrating as no sex. But goddamn if it was not cathartic. Putting words to paper was more freeing than anything he had ever felt. He played sports and enjoyed the physicality of throwing his body around. It was regulated violence. But nothing was as cathartic as being able to express thoughts and ideas without anyone else's control. He could throw verbal punches against everything that was oppressing him. Words were powerful. They could also be weak and delicate. Sometimes that was what he wanted. He wanted his full range of emotion to flow out of him. It was not polite in real life to let loose and scream when you are angry or cry when you are sad. People look at you strangely on the bus. Sometimes they ask you to get off. No, what was freeing, to Jonathan, was that there were no rules imposed on him. Even grammar, structure and spelling change over time. Who knew what Bill Shakespeare would think of the twenty first century? He'd probably have his own blog, that's for sure. He'd rant and rave about how no one is going to see his plays. No, let's be honest, he'd probably not write stage plays. It's a cute medium but it's not the one for the masses that his work in the Elizabethan era was aimed at. He'd write screenplays for blockbuster movies. They would have explosions and sex and include some really awful crude lines, and the occasional philosophical joke thrown out as a cue to the smarter members of the audience that he knows exactly what he is doing. Shakespeare would be a sell out.

Jonathan didn't want to sell out. He didn't want billions of dollars and a direct line to Michael Bay. He was quite comfortable living in his life of champagne squalor. Then he checked his email. Greeting him there was a notification that he'd received a royalty payment for his first novel. It was for $11.32. It was going to be an uphill battle to even think about having to turn down calls from Michael Bay wanting to turn his ensemble drama in to an action buddy comedy with car chases. The really sad part about his royalty payment was that it covered the past six months. Six months. In six months he had made $11.32 selling his writing. He made twice that every hour he showed up for work. The danger of becoming a best selling author was really not on the horizon. On the bright side he could afford one six pack of Belgian beer with that payment, one beer for every month. Jonathan began to think about whether he wanted to get Leffe Brun or Blonde. It was always a toss up.

Outside his window, yelling interrupted Jonathan's thoughts. There was the occasional disturbance in the neighbourhood, but it was usually just a couple yelling at each other as they passed by. It only served to underscore Jonathan's loneliness. This was not the case as the yelling persisted and it was only coming from one source. There was the crazy guy in the basement; it could have been him. Jonathan found him a bit off, and every time he had to go down to do his laundry he had the fear that he would run in to him.

One time when he was loading his clothes in to the washer, Jonathan saw the crazy guy roll in to the laundry room on an office chair. The man rolled up to the vending machine and purchased a can of pop. When he reached in to pick up the can from the slot at the bottom of the machine, he let out a horrible yelp. Jonathan looked up expecting to see that the man had got his limb jammed in the slot and desperate for help. Instead he saw the door to the laundry room close shut and the sound of the wheels on the office chair squeak down the hall.

Still, the screaming persisted outside his window and Jonathan knew that it was not coming from the basement. He looked out to see with astonishment four police squad cars lined in the street. Up against the trunk of one of the cars was a large man who was letting loose a torrent of verbal abuse on the officers. Jonathan was relieved to see that the handcuffed man's face was not familiar. He had no idea who this man was or what he was doing outside his apartment. Jonathan could only hear the unintelligible screams of the man as he fired bulleted words at his captors. Jonathan tried to count the number of police officers and settled on four, possibly five. It might have been only four if each officer rode alone in their squad car. Evidently this man was either an extremely dangerous criminal or these officers had nothing else to do on this otherwise quiet Thursday night. Jonathan hoped that it was the latter and not the former.

With the captive screamer quietly placed in the back of the squad car and the four officers laughing and joking about it outside, Jonathan safely assumed that there really was nothing too serious going on. He returned to his computer and tried to continue writing his story.

The Couch

Jonathan's forehead pounded with increasing frequency. Thump, thump thump, thump thump thump, thump thump thump thump, thud. He was out.

He awoke with the glaze of the sun beaming in his window and onto his face. Its warmth was welcome and Jonathan sighed contently. He loved mornings like these, when there was nowhere in particular to be, no one in particular to see, nothing in particular to do. Sunday mornings were a blessing, as intended for a day of rest. Nothing could motivate Jonathan to move or start his day any sooner. Ha, what was there to start? He smiled knowing that he didn't have to move until Monday.

An agitated doorbell rang repeatedly; impatiently waiting to be answered it was joined by a thunderous knock knock knock knock. Jon would have to leave Shangri La after all. Opening the door in his bare feet, plaid pyjama bottoms and t-shirt Jonathan was greeted by the familiarly irritated face of his slumlord.

The majority of the little university town was divided among only a handful of inattentive landlords, each with their own flaws. There were sex perverts, drug addicts and misers. Jonathan's landlord happened to be a miserly drug addict. Any sexual deviancy was well hidden, if applicable. The circumstances, however, of how he came in to possession of over one hundred rental units in such a small town was unknown, but the fact that he was able to maintain ownership despite his largest vice was remarkable. He was a horrible old soot on his own but made all the worse by the stimulants he inhaled.

"Why is there a couch in the garbage?"

"Sorry, what?"

"In the garbage. The bin. There is a couch in the garbage. Why?"

Jonathan knew exactly why, but was not going to say a thing. The old bastard ought to be happy it was in the garbage and nowhere else.

"There is a couch in the garbage?"

"Well, I should say there is what was a couch in the garbage."

"So, there is not a couch in the garbage?"

"No it's there. But it's no longer there."

"I don't understand. How can it be there and not be there?"

"There was a couch and now it's in the garbage."

"What's in the garbage?"

"A couch."

"Oh, so there is a couch in the garbage?"

"Yes. And no."

"So what's in the garbage?"

"A couch."

"Well, if there is a couch in the garbage why are you at my door?"

"This is my door."

"Then why am I on the inside?"

"I rent this to you."

"So it's mine, for now."

"But the couch "

"Is in the garbage."

"Yes."

"But it's not in the garbage."

"No, it's in the garbage but it's no more."

"You mean no longer. In English we properly say no longer rather than no more."

"It's still there."

"Then you are mistaken. I'm sorry for the misunderstanding."

Jonathan went to close the door on the old man.

"Wait, I ask you about the couch."

"I thought we agreed it's in the garbage."

"And it's no more."

"No longer."

"Yes it's still there, but it's no more, the couch."

"The couch is no longer."

"It's still there!"

"Then what are you asking me about?"

"Why is it there? And why is it no more?"

"Rene, do you realise you are asking me two different questions?"

"Why is the couch there?"

"Which couch?"

"The couch in the garbage."

"I thought it was no longer there."

"It's there. It's no more."

Jonathan tried to hide his pleasure with this encounter. He felt some pangs of guilt for messing around with the sponge brain of an elderly cokehead, but knowing that in all likelihood his monthly rent went towards the jerk's habit balanced the experience out.

"Well which is it?"

"It's there and it's no more."

"That's not a choice."

"What do you know about the couch?"

"Only what you have told me. It was in the garbage but now it's no longer."

"Wrong, I said it's in the garbage and it's no more."

"Why are you asking me about this?"

"I believe this is your couch."

"No, my couch is in my living room. See, look."

A couch sat within view of the door. Rene eyed it suspiciously as if it might have been responsible for the couch in the garbage that was no more.

"You have another couch."

"No, it's actually more of a futon. A bit awkward to sit on, we keep a bed sheet on it in case of spills, you know how roommates can be. You don't have roommates do you? You know I have three. You leased this place to us. Anyways, the futon acts like a couch most of the time, it's good at role-play, but occasionally we ask it to be a bed. It swings both ways, Rene, you understand? It's great for guests."

"You have another couch."

"No, that's it. Nick, I think, has a futon in his room, too. You remember Nick? He was the tall, broad one from Nova Scotia. He does not use it for guests, but I suppose he could easily convert it for that purpose. It's practically the same as the one in our living room. Futons are futons, by all accounts."

"What about the couch in the garbage?"

"I thought you said it was in the garbage but it's no longer."

"It's no more."

"Right. We agreed on that bit, Rene."

"I think that couch in the garbage is yours."

"Well what colour is it?"

"It does not have a colour."

"That's a bit ridiculous, everything has a colour."

"It used to have a colour."

"Well what colour did it used to have?"

"I don't know."

"How can you say that a couch that has no colour, that used to have an unknown colour, that's in the garbage but it is no longer could possibly be mine?"

"I think it is."

"Look over there, there is my couch. It's brown. I can see that. You can see that. That, over there, is my couch."

"I believe you had another couch and you put it in the garbage last night."

"If I put it in the garbage last night, why would it no longer be there?"

"It is no more."

"So what's the problem?"

"It's in the garbage."

"I thought it was no longer."

"It is no more."

"You keep repeating yourself, Rene. I don't know if this is a language barrier between us, but if it helps I will go get Gio to translate."

With that suggestion Jon went upstairs and found Gio, filled him in on the situation and brought him down to the door to speak to Rene. The patience of the old man at this point was shot and he let out a tirade of abuse at Gio, waving his arms back and forth, pointing at Jon and then the dumpster behind their building. Finally after what seemed like five minutes he paused and let Gio relay the message.

"He says somebody burned a couch in the lot last night and threw the charred remains in the dumpster."

Jonathan was deeply amused by all of this.

"Oh, so that's what you meant, Rene. I get it. It's no more. Really interesting stuff. The thing is, though, that it wasn't us and that's not our couch. As you can see our living room is pretty full right now with a couch and a futon as it is. There wouldn't be any room for another."

"So that was not your couch."

"No, you can have my word, that couch was not mine."

"Okay, well give me a call if you find out anything more."

"I will give you a call, Rene, the moment any new information comes to light on this."

The old junkie stumbled down the stairs and got in his pickup truck, spreading gravel in all directions as he quickly drove away.

"That was close, Jon."

"That was hilarious, Gio."

The night before had been one of catharsis and end of summer revelry. At their new apartment, the boys had hosted some of their friends from first year in residence. It had been a long summer since they had seen many of them and moving off campus had brought with it a feeling of freedom. It had also created an opportunity to try new things and to test new boundaries. What was acceptable had been rewritten. Under the archaic restrictions of the university housing czar perfectly normal rites of passage had been forbidden. Out on the new frontiers of college, living in a privately rented accommodation, it was the Wild West. Gio was Billy the Kid and Jon was Jesse James. Their antics were befitting of a night pounding moonshine whiskey and playing cards outside the OK Corral. Instead of moonshine whiskey it was cheap domestic lager and instead of playing cards it was setting fire to a couch after it had been tossed off a balcony. There was no reason to riot, but goddamn those kids did. No one claimed ownership of the couch. It didn't belong to any of the four of them; Jon, Gio, Nick or Drew. This was an outsider and it needed to get the fuck out. The previous tenants had left it behind and had no interest in returning for it. They had moved out four months ago, and to everyone's knowledge had likely all graduated. They didn't have any need for an ugly old couch that had probably seen a lifetime's worth of blood, semen, vomit and urine. Jon couldn't remember who suggested it, to throw the damn thing out, but when he came back from grabbing a beer from the fridge, the place he had been sitting was hanging off the edge of the balcony. Nick and Drew were holding onto the ends while they could hear Gio and some others giving instruction. Jon put down his beer and ran outside to watch it fall. It hit the ground with a loud snapping sound, followed by the cheers of a dozen drunk and high boys and the gasps of the few girls in the crowd. Without instruction the guys starting attacking the couch, beating their enemy with whatever tools they could fashion. At first it started with some of them kicking at the frame, but once they had cracked loose parts, those became tools to inflict pain upon the body from where they once came. Then, just as their violence could only climax, flames burst up from the corpse of the unwanted sofa. Jon held the lighter in his hand and emitted a perverse laugh. Not wanting to be a part of what was surely a fineable offence, the majority of the crowd retreated back in to the apartment, leaving Jon, Nick and Gio to watch the couch die alone. Jon suggested they lift it up while they still could and the three boys hoisted it in to the dumpster. Parts of the couch were still lit and slowly charred away at the rest.

"Fuck, that got out of hand really quick."

"Yeah, but it felt great."

"Yup. It really did."

"Do you think anyone is going to have a problem with this?"

"I can think of several."

"Oh well."

The boys went back inside and rejoined their own party. The Bacchanalian atmosphere was infectious and everyone danced into themselves, forgetting temporarily the stupidity pyre outside. They were young and foolish, drunk on life, living without limits, and it suited them just fine in that moment.

Seven

-Hi, Jonathan? It's Eliza.

-Hey Eliza, how are you?

-I'm good. How are you?

-I'm fine.

-You didn't get back to me about coffee.

-Oh, sorry, yeah, I totally forgot.

-You do that a lot.

-Yeah, I know.

-How is your writing coming along?

-It's coming along.

-I think I told you already, but I liked your book.

-Yeah, thanks. I appreciate that.

-You are a really good writer. You should keep up with it.

-Haha, thanks Eliza, I'm trying.

The email notification about his royalty payment kept running through Jonathan's head. $11.32 was what being a really good writer was worth these days.

-How's work going?

-It's the same as always, you?

-I'm really enjoying it.

-That's good.

-Yeah, it's.

-Yeah.

-So, did you want to do coffee?

-Oh, yeah, sorry I forgot again.

-What night are you free?

Jonathan looked at his calendar and only saw targeted word counts.

-Any night. What works for you?

-Let's meet Wednesday.

-Okay, Wednesday it's.

-Our favourite place?

-Yeah, for sure.

-See you then, Jonathan.

-See you Wednesday, Eliza. Bye.

Jonathan hated the ritual. Every time he wanted to meet with Eliza he would inevitably end up in a conversation about her and her boyfriend. He had nothing against the guy. He was by all accounts a great guy. He was a great boyfriend. Eliza was happy. It all made sense for her and him. It didn't help Jonathan out at all, though. He didn't want to be selfish, but he wanted things to be better for him. For once he wanted to go out for coffee with a friend and go on and on about how he's found the perfect person, that they had bought a dog, and a house, and were talking about marriage. He wanted those things. And he wanted that friend that he was having coffee with to be secretly lusting about him. Jonathan wanted things to be the opposite from what they were. This ritual was due for an end. Jonathan was not a jerk, though. He had no intention of ever trying to break up other people. That's their own life and he has no right to interfere, whether they are happy or not. Even if it would help break his own loneliness, Jonathan couldn't bring himself to make a grand declaration of love, for fear that in the end he might be worse for her than who she has. All he could do was continue to perform the ritual.

"So, the pope is dead."

The class looked up as the absurd professor entered the room. John Paul II had reportedly passed away the day before and it was consuming the airwaves. Jon had watched the procession of mourners pay their respects outside St. Peter's but felt unmoved. He was not Catholic. Neither, it seems, was his philosophy professor.

"Good morning, class, I see you are all alive, that's more than can be said for John Paul."

Jon was unmoved by the death, but he had not lost a certain amount of reverence and decorum that certain figures and institutions demanded. Not yet, anyways.

"I was flipping through the channels last night and it was everywhere, John Paul is dead. It's a shame, but there were programs I wanted to watch. They were all pre empted. It will be a week before things get back to usual."

This class was easily one of Jon's favourites, if not entirely for the irreverent professor. He was a man who was unafraid to say what he thought. Tenure was a beautiful thing.

"I finally ended up watching pornography. It was the only thing not kowtowing to popery."

With that, the discussion turned to the mechanisms of sexual intercourse, whether it has any meaning in modern or post-modern life.

"It's like going to a vending machine, sex, and punching in E5 to get your cheesy crisps. That's what sex is. It has no more meaning than that. It's just a function of what we do. I sleep. I eat. I fart. I poop. I have sex. None of these are profound acts."

Jon looked around at the sheepish looks on the faces of his classmates. Three days earlier, on Saturday night he had seen most of them at the bar. They were all looking to score. They, and he, and everyone else were always looking to score. Sex apparently had lost any sort of higher meaning, if it ever had one, but it still remained their primary concern.

"Say a man, and a woman, or two men, or two women, or a man and a horse, I don't know, whichever way you want to imagine it. Say the man and his partner, who could be a woman, or a man, or a horse, say they want to have sex. They do. That's it. There is no special ceremony, they don't need to lay out beautiful rose petals down the hallway to get the man erect, he just needs to know he is having sex and he is good to go. It's no different than eating. If I want to eat, I just eat. It does not have to be a Thanksgiving dinner, with special meanings, and we gather around all our friends and family, who we don't like, and say a special prayer and all the nice things that have happened before we eat the turkey. If we want turkey we just eat turkey."

As usual the students had little clue what the professor was rambling on about. His words were enjoyable to listen to, they all agreed, even if they didn't sink in.

"Sex is like that. I watched a porno film last night and I tell you it was refreshing. They don't try to dance around the main interest of the characters. Even when the woman has a broken sink or toilet, and the plumber man comes to fix it, she does not tell him to go fix the sink or toilet. She wants sex! And, not surprisingly, the plumber man, even though he probably has lots of other house calls to make to other housewives with broken sinks and toilets, he wants sex, too. They have sex, the housewife and the plumber man. That's it."

It was all so straightforward. Jon wanted sex too. Within the room there were eight girls and he could admit that he wanted to have sex with each of them. He looked at the old professor and believed the same thoughts were in his mind too. Next to Jon was his friend Jerry and he knew, as he had heard it many times, that Jerry also wanted to have sex with each of those eight girls. No special ceremony was needed.

For all the talk about not needing any special ceremony, it still seemed that culturally there were rituals that did need to be observed to have sex. Men couldn't be complete brutes and just walk up and ask if a girl wanted to fuck. They had to say hello, and ask her name first, maybe even take her out for a coffee.

Jonathan felt sick writing the words. He was not getting any pleasure out of it anymore. It was not about Eliza, specifically. It was every girl that got away. The chase had always been so easy before. He could win them over with his charm and capture them for what seemed like a fading moment, a shooting star. Jonathan could catch and romance any girl at the start. It was always the follow through that sucked. That night Jonathan was haunted in his dreams by what seemed like every girl he had ever known. The scenes where they met would run through his mind. Those were always something special. That first spark was always felt. They were followed in his mind by the happy middle part, the part where, for however brief, Jonathan was with them. Scenes of domestic bliss made up the majority of those moments. Sitting on a couch, curled up, watching a movie or a hockey game, eating buttery popcorn. Jonathan tried as much as he could in his dreams to slow those parts down, but his mind wouldn't let him. There was a destination these dreams all had to get to and they had a pace set to reach it on time. Sure enough, the ends of every relationship Jonathan Jones had ever been in cascaded through his head. He woke in a cold sweat. It was two in the morning and Jonathan's heart was pumping irregularly. He could barely breathe.

-I told you I'm asthmatic.

Sorry, I know, I just wanted to detail the extent of how much that dream had affected you.

-Real kind of you.

Jonathan sat up on the side of his bed and brought his breathing to a more controlled tempo. He stood up and walked in to his kitchen and steadily drank a glass of water. There was no way he could get back to sleep now. Jonathan sat down at his desk and turns on his laptop. While waiting for the computer to turn on, Jonathan jots a few notes down on his pad of paper. With his word processor open, the middle of the night typing commences.

"Hi."

"Hi."

"What are you drinking?"

"I think it's merlot."

"Oh, any good?"

"I don't really know any different, to be honest. I'm new to wine."

"Yeah, me too."

"I think I have only really drank it at these wine and cheeses."

"Hah, me too. It's funny, because I don't think any one else knows any more about wine than us, either."

"No, probably not."

"The professors could probably save some of their money by buying the cheap bottles at the SAQ."

"I can't tell the difference."

"Me neither. Seven or twenty dollars is just a gap of thirteen dollars. They could buy more cheese with that."

"Or crackers that don't fall apart."

"I know! I have had like six crumble in my hand while I try to spread on some of this gourmet cheese. I think it's Norwegian or something."

"Oh, the blue cheese?"

"Yeah."

"I think that's Norwegian. I don't really like blue cheese."

"No?"

"Isn't it rotten on purpose?"

"I don't think rotten is the right word for it. It's delicious though."

"I have never tried it."

"I thought you said you don't really like blue cheese."

"Well, I'm guessing I wouldn't really like it."

"Do you do that often, guess about things without giving them a chance?"

"I'm trying to be very open minded these days."

"If a friendly guy started talking to you at a wine and cheese would you give him a chance?"

"I might. Depends on whether or not he has blue cheese on his breath."

"Which you've never tasted."

"True, and I don't think it's going to be today that I do."

Jon was smitten. This girl was witty and very attractive.

"What's your name?"

"Veronica."

"Like in the comics?"

"Yes, and you must be Archie."

"Haha, I hope so. I'm Jonathan."

"Very nice to meet you, Jonathan."

She drank the wine that they believed to be merlot and talked to him for almost an hour. It was one of those uninterrupted conversations that just seemed to flow from one subject to another. Jon discovered all sorts of things about her, but still wanted to know more. That's the powerful thing about attraction; it has no limit to its strength. Even when you think there is no possible way to feel the pull of the magnet any further, you get knocked off your feet. Veronica had a way of doing that without saying a word. There was something about her and the way she stood that made Jon infatuated instantly. How could he possibly resist? It was a silly thought for him to even think that he could. No man could. It's not in their constitution to fight the pull of attraction.

Eight

-Hey Jonathan.

Eliza looked absolutely gorgeous. In the winter weather she had worn a brightly coloured scarf and a dark gray peacoat. The cold air had given her cheeks a nice red hue.

-Hi Eliza.

-You've got a mustache!

-Oh, right, I forgot to tell you that I was doing this.

-It suits you.

-People have said that. I don't know what that means.

-You look very distinguished.

-Ha, I hardly feel distinguished.

-You are an author; that's distinguished.

-Um, sure, I will take your compliment. Thank you.

He wondered if everyone who wrote a book was considered distinguished by others. There were a lot of truly awful writers, outnumbered only by their vices. Were they distinguished? Did they have mustaches?

-But, seriously, you do look good.

-Thank you, you always look good, Eliza.

-Thanks.

Why keep mentioning their respective attractiveness, Jonathan wondered. What good could come from this? It was torturous for him to even have to sit and look at such a lovely creature, but to have to make small talk about her looks, that was unbearable.

-So, you said that you are really enjoying work?

-Yes, I'm. It's been amazing. I have only been working there a short time and they are already giving me more responsibilities.

-Oh, cool. What sort of things?

-Well, you know I can't talk about specific files, but they are letting me do more and more on the analysis side.

-Right, you were doing administrative work before.

-Yeah, but they know that where I really want to be is on the analysis side, actually looking at policy.

-That's why you went to school.

-Right, exactly.

-So, do you think there is a lot of room for you to grow there or do you think you might move on elsewhere at some point?

-I like it where I'm at, the people are great, and I really think that there is the potential for me to move up and do a lot more than what I'm doing.

-Yeah, you are obviously more than capable.

-Thanks. I don't feel like that every day. There are still small mistakes that I'm making.

-Sure, but you will figure those out in no time.

-I hope so. My boss seems to like me.

-That's good. That's the first thing, right?

-Yeah, I think so.

-I'm glad to hear you are enjoying it.

-How about you, Jonathan?

-Ah, I don't know. It's a job.

-Do you like it?

-Yes, yeah, I like my job.

-That's good.

-I guess.

-What do you mean you guess?

-Well, I just think that it's a job and not really a vocation. You know?

-I don't know. This is what we went to school for, is not it?

-Well, sort of, yeah. But I'm not sure I went to school for this. I think I might have gone to school in this, but not for it.

-I'm confused.

-So am I, but it's a bit late for that.

-Is it?

-Yeah, I don't know that this is what I want to do with the rest of my life.

-No, you probably don't. But you are smart and capable and could do it.

-That's the problem. I think other people see me doing this more than I see myself doing it.

-You look like a bureaucrat.

She smiled with a look that let Jonathan know that she was only joking. He didn't want to admit it to her then, but that smile nearly killed him.

-Haha, thanks. You are a real friend.

-It's what I do.

-Good, don't stop doing that any time soon.

-I don't think you'd let me.

-No, it's true.

-Every time I try to disappear, you have a habit of showing up again.

-Likewise.

-Have you read any good books lately?

-Yeah, a bit. Hmm, let's see, what were some recent ones I liked? Have you heard of the *White Tiger*? It was really good.

-The name sounds familiar.

-Yeah, I really enjoyed that one. Also, *A Fraction of the Whole*. It's ridiculously funny and ridiculously well written. I actually stopped writing for six weeks after reading it.

-Really?

-Yeah, Toltz, the guy who wrote it, basically destroys any hope I can have of being even a good author. He frightens me.

-What? Seriously?

-It was his debut novel and it was probably the best book I have read written in the last ten years. I'm scared to think what he is capable of in the future.

-Your book was good, too!

-Thanks, Eliza, I appreciate that, but seriously my book was something awful compared to Toltz.

-But you are working on something new, right?

-Yeah, I have started writing something.

-What's it about?

-It's supposed to be a comedy. I want to write about the university experience and all the wild things that happen.

-Oh, wow, that sounds cool! You should have lots of things to write about. You and your friends always had the craziest stories.

-Thanks, Eliza. That's the idea.

-Well when you are done I want to read it, okay?

-Sure, no problem. If it's not completely terrible I will let you read it.

-I'm sure it won't be. You really are a good writer.

-Is it my turn to pay for coffee?

-I think it might be.

-Great, I will get this.

The bill came to $9.03. Jonathan was a little amused that despite his being a really good writer, two gourmet coffees had made a significant dent in to six months worth of writing. Whatever happened to artists having patrons? Where was an aristocrat when you need one, Jonathan thought.

Nine

Meeting with Eliza always gave Jonathan a foul mood afterwards. Sure enough, she had talked about her current and future plans with her boyfriend. It was not really the kind of uplifting talk that he wanted to hear. Nothing makes a miserable person more miserable than hearing about the good fortunes of others. This time it was about their romantic vacation in the New Year to some Caribbean resort. Perfect, Jonathan thought, just another online photo album to lust angrily over.

He did appreciate Eliza's kind words about his writing, but it was always hard with friends to gauge how honest they were being. What friend would stop another from pursuing their dream, no matter how ridiculous it's? Delusion is not built on lies, but untold truths.

Jonathan felt miserable. At the bottom of his fridge were twelve beers. He took out one and flopped himself on his couch. Flicking on the television he sat bored and depressed. Seeing how beautiful Eliza was in person was painful. Every single time it reopened scabs that Jonathan had thought healed a half decade ago. He wanted his mind to wander anywhere else.

-This fucking sucks.

He scanned the listings on the screen for any and all distractions he could find. Television was a vast wasteland of nothingness and Jonathan wanted to enter it as deep as his mind would allow. There was no shortage of options, each as repulsive as the next. He clicked on to one of the sports channels, to watch the evening's highlights. They were showing clips about American football and Jonathan's disinterest in the sport wouldn't let him get sucked in. Foiled, he thought. He began to press the channel up button in the hopes that he would just stumble across anything that might pique his interest and distract him. There were makeover programs for frumpy office workers and documentaries about Iraq, cartoon episodes he had seen a thousand times and talk shows he never wanted to watch, in the end Jonathan came across the worst possible thing to watch. In front of him was a vapid group of twenty somethings on a reality show, treating each other like shit. They cussed at each other. They drank too much. They were the absolute bottom rung of society's evolutionary progress. They were Neanderthals with spray tans. But Jonathan couldn't look away. He was drawn in to how stupid and petty they were. How unambitious their dreams were. The only thing any of them wanted to do was party and have a good time. Jonathan was not having a good time. He was alone on his couch and already his first beer was empty. He grabbed another and continued to watch these despicable beasts fight and fuck. The beers continued to disappear and the episodes kept coming. Jonathan had stumbled across a marathon of vacuity. He let his mind get sucked in.

The Contest

Jonathan wanted to scream out "don't do it!" at the graduating students as they crossed the stage, as if they were about to jump off a building. He was afraid that none of them knew what they were doing. They were signing on to the rest of their lives. It was not going to be filled with bikinis and shots at the beach. It was going to be filled with an endless march of paperwork and bullshit. He wanted them to know what they would be missing. He wanted to remind them that before their end, there were so many stories. He wanted to remind them of the time that Gio walked across the top of the bridge's arches and nearly fell ("It was crazy!"). Or when Gio saw the passing train and jumped and held on to the ladder hanging from the side, his legs dangerously dangling below ("Do you remember?"). Jonathan wanted to scream at the top of his lungs that this was the end of mindless shenanigans. He looked around and knew several of these suited corpses were already working for banks and non-profits. He saw some of his classmates who he knew were destined for graduate school. That wouldn't stop this death, he wanted to warn them, it's just a slower way to go. He wanted to remind them all that there were beginnings to this, there was a time when they were not even fully who they are now. Jonathan, sitting in silent frustration, began to remind himself.

"'A group of us on the floor, Nick, Gio, Midge, Whatsherface, and myself clicked early and formed a core. While we all had disparate backgrounds there was one common bond that brought us together. In a familiar refrain from just about every university retrospective, that bond was drinking. Alcohol found itself at the centre of just about any gathering of the five of us. Whether we were in Midge's room, laughing hysterically at the mislabeled songs on her computer ("Don't Worry, Be Happy" is not performed by Bob Marley), or having Nick introduce us to the works of Raoul Duke in film, alcohol was omnipresent. It became pretty clear that within the five of us there were varying degrees of skill and tolerance with the liquid devil. Midge was a lightweight, not helped at all by her preference for light domestic beers. On the other end of the spectrum was Whatsherface, who could consume an ungodly amount of rum and hold her own with the boys well in to the night, at which point she would finally collapse. I was never a heavyweight, and I always foolishly tried to punch above my weight in those early days. It would begin with a decision to match Gio and Nick and it would end with a toilet bowl. No, there was no question that Gio and Nick were supremely gifted in the art, craft, skill, trade, and game of drinking. You name it; they could do it. If it was a punishing round of cards, randomly flipped over with various disciplinary actions, those two would down their poison without hesitation. They would be playing flip cup and they'd not chug a beer but gulp in one fell swallow. Of course, their flipping only matched their drinking. At the pub one night, Nick decided to order a pitcher of beer — for himself. Gio matched him. While us remaining mugs filled pint glasses from a common pitcher, Gio and Nick drank straight from their own jugs. By the end of the night each had drank four or five jugs, depending on who was counting.

And that was the problem between the two; there was never an agreement about who was best. So, to solve this, and I cannot be entirely certain as to the exact origin, but I suspect that alcohol was at play, Gio and Nick agreed to a duel. It sounded old timey and quaint and was exactly the sort of thing young gentlemen ought to do when honour is on the line.

The terms to the duel were agreed on a Friday morning in the residence food hall over breakfast. Nick was devouring a mountain of eggs and bacon, while Gio sipped coffee and stared at a platter of pancakes.

"A drink-a-thon."

Nick's face lit up at the idea of testing his booze endurance. Gio sipped his coffee nonplussed. I continued to explain the terms of the challenge.

"Starting tomorrow morning at nine you will both begin to drink, keeping tally of how many you consume. Whoever drinks the most by midnight will win. If for whatever reason you cannot complete the drink a thon, for whatever reason, the other person will win. Are these terms clear?"

I reveled in the possibility of being the referee, for it meant that for once I was not expected to keep up in the drinking. It was incumbent upon the drink a thon commissioner to keep a level head on the proceedings.

"Aww, man, this is gonna hurt."

"Haha, Gio, you are gonna collapse!"

Nick began to feel more confident as he surveyed the mindboggling frame of his opponent. Gio was a tall, skinny fellow of questionable origins. He smoked a pack of cigarettes per day and was not known to participate in any form of exercise. Still, when being generous you would describe his body as being that of a runner, and runners ran marathons.

That day, as I attended classes, all I could think about was the challenge. I honestly wanted to know who could consume more alcohol in a horrible fifteen-hour session. I suppose there is a masochist in each of us. When I returned to the residence for the evening Nick was at my door.

"Hey, Jon, you wanna have a drink?"

"Yeah, I could, what about tomorrow?"

"I'm training."

There was always a way to find yourself agreeing with Nick. This was training. Runners don't just walk up to a marathon and then out of nowhere run the distance. They prepare themselves for weeks or months on end. They learn to pace themselves. They can tell you within a few minutes how long a forty-kilometre run is going to take them. The remarkable accuracy came from finely tuning their bodies so that they were as reliable and predictable as an automobile. Nick was a truck. He powered through *drink like large imposing figures ought to. Thinking of automobiles, I couldn't quite place Gio. Was he an economy class Hyundai Accent? Or some obscure European vehicle? He was a stretch limousine with a VW Beetle face, leather seats, zebra print interior and Motley Crue blasting through the speakers.*

I couldn't believe we were training that night. Nick insisted I keep up with him, so one drink became twelve and we were still at the residence. I had rarely drank so much in a pre drinking session and was already feeling a horrible buzz. Gio was nowhere to be found that night. I don't know if he hibernated in preparation for the challenge but he was not joining Nick and I that night.

I looked at my watch; it was only eight. Somehow we had managed to consume twelve beers each in the span of two and a half hours. This is the time when someone's heart ought to explode. Nick just motoring along without any hesitation. It really was training for him. I had made the mistake of jogging next to a marathoner. For me this was a hobby, for Nick it was a lifestyle. If he had the ambition to be a rock star I'm fairly certain all the other members of the band would hold an intervention about his alcohol use. Instead of warning him about the inevitable harm he was doing, I think his band would tell him to tone it down a bit because he was making the rest of them look bad. That's the thing with rock bands; everyone in the same band wants to be thought of the same way. It's why aging "boy bands", with men in their thirties or forties, really are creepy.

"Let's go to Klub Karaoke."

Damn Nick. He always knew the right thing to say. Klub Karaoke was this tiny hole in the wall biker gang bar we had discovered just down the road from the main strip of clubs and pubs downtown. Its usual occupancy was about four people, with three of them gruff looking members. Nick liked going there to brighten the place up. In the month or so we had been at university at that point, Nick, Gio, myself and some other guys we knew had collectively been to Klub Karaoke two times before.

The first had involved Nick's heart warming rendition of Hootie and the Blowfish's seminal "Let Her Cry", with the small modification of swapping out the proper lyrics, which Nick may not have been able to read from the screen in front of him at that point in the night, and swapping in as many expletives as he could think of. "Fucking, you fucking fuck face, cock blasters, I fucking hope you die in a shitty pile of fucking rubble, assholes" had never sounded so angrily charming. Afterwards, Nick collapsed facedown on the table, but insisted he was just resting his eyes. That was the same night, when without any intended form of irony or satire, I chose to sing the Eric Clapton version of "Cocaine". I belted the whole thing out and to my tone deaf, drunken ears; I thought I did a pretty stand up job. When I returned to the table Nick was not impressed. He had a frightened – though bemused – look on his face.

"I think we need to get going."

"Why?"

"You just fucking sang "Cocaine"."

"So?"

"There was literally a cocaine deal exchanged at the bar while you were at the mic."

"Really?"

"Yeah, really. I don't think they were too impressed with your choice of song."

"How did I sound?"

"Awful. Truly awful."

"Excellent, let's go."

I still don't know whether a cocaine deal actually transpired, or whether Nick and Gio had got themselves in to a situation at the table while I was blissfully belting out "Cocaine". The look of the biker nearest our table, a portly fellow with a handlebar mustache was certainly not friendly. Nick had began to space out at whatever he was looking at, and had likely stared at the biker's lady, a cheetah clad cougar. We got up and started walking out of the bar. Every face followed us to the door. It was no mistake. We really did need to leave.

The second time we went to Klub Karaoke was a week after the first. A haze surrounded the whole evening. I remember black lights. Techno music. And a sudden, panicked intervention from Nick informing me that we had been kicked out for reasons to be explained later. I cheerfully finished my Labatt 50 and moved on with the evening. Nick mentioned something about broken bottles and a fire alarm.

And now, on the eve of the drink a thon challenge between Nick and Gio, Nick had decided to head back to Klub Karaoke. We walked across the campus grounds, planning to make our way to the front of the campus and catch a taxi there. The twelve Heinekens I had drunk to keep pace with Nick were really starting to hit. I had neither the experience nor the composition to handle that much beer in such a short span. We neared the front of the campus and were about to hop in a taxi when my body forced me to pause. I leaned against a wall and let vomit pour out against the brick in front of me and the asphalt below. Relieved, and somewhat more settled I hopped in the cab.

"Dude, you just puked on a church."

"Huh?"

I looked out the window of the taxi and saw the silhouette of the campus chapel. I was not sure whether I had committed any particular form of sacrilege, but I certainly agreed that it was, at the very least, rude to vomit on the side of any building, religious or secular.

At Klub Karaoke that night was an unusual multitude of patrons. Inside, Nick and I sat in the corner and watched as the Quebecoise danced their little butts off, while their orangutan boyfriends laughed over forty ounce bottles of cheap domestic. This was not the normal biker crowd, but these folks were not students either. These were people with real jobs and low expectations.

Nick continued to pound down the beers with ease. I don't remember if I had even touched mine. I knew I had ordered at least one because I had done it at the bar, embarrassingly so, by trying to flirt with the bartender. She was having none of it. To be fair, I likely was not throwing anything sexy out at her anyways. I was still the man who had puked on the side of the campus chapel within the hour. Did I chew any gum? I think I had. I checked my pockets but didn't find a pack. Nick must have given me some.

I went outside for some air and walked around the corner. My hands rested on my knees and I leaned over to prepare myself for further vomiting. Nothing came out. Saliva dripped from my lips and formed a small puddle on the concrete. I stood up, cleared whatever saliva stuck to the sides of my mouth and walked back towards the bar.

Outside the front door stood a woman smoking a cigarette. She was probably in her early thirties. She was wearing tight jeans and had a down vest over her blouse. I smiled stupidly at her as I went to walk back in to the bar.

"Hello."

She spoke. It was a rather strange shock.

"Um, hello."

"Do you speak English or French?"

"English."

"What's your name?"

"Jonathan."

"You are very cute, Jonathan."

I didn't feel very cute. She grabbed my hand and pulled me away from the door and had me stand next to her as she finished her cigarette.

"What are you doing here, Jonathan?"

"At the bar?"

"No, in general."

What a strange way to word it.

"I'm a student."

"What do you study?"

"History."

"Very interesting, I like history."

"Oh."

This was the extent of our very interesting conversation. When she finished her cigarette she grabbed me again and pulled me against her down vest and planted her mouth on mine. We kissed for maybe a minute or two and then she reached in to her purse and on the back of a receipt wrote down her phone number.

"You call?"

She re-entered the bar at the same time that Nick came out to find me.

"Hey, how's it going? Did you puke again?"

"No, but I did just make out with that woman."

Nick looked back and saw the down vest disappear in to Klub Karaoke.

"Awesome."

On the cab ride back we couldn't settle on whether I had actually chewed any gum that evening. It was two in the morning, which in those days was actually fairly early, but Nick and I both agreed that considering he had to start drinking for fifteen hours at nine some sleep might be helpful. I decided to swallow about a litre of water and collapse on my bed.

The next morning when my alarm went off I was thankful for thinking to hydrate myself. After all that alcohol, not to mention the purging, it does the body good to ensure it does not turn in to the Gobi overnight.

Nick was not in good shape at all that morning. Gio had alerted me to his awakening by flicking on his stereo, letting Guns 'N Roses blast, and hopping in the shower. Nick, on the other hand needed some prompting to join the living world. When we started slandering his masculinity and raising the possibility of declaring Gio the winner, then and there, that's when the door finally opened. Wearing his samurai sandal look (white socks and flip-flops), boxers and a hooded sweater, the Pride of Dartmouth opened the door.

"Let's do this."

Gio, looking fresh from his shower and likely having not debauched himself in the same manner as we had last night, handed Nick a bottle of Ex. Their eyes met, heads nodded in agreement, bottle tops were tipped, and down the hatch went the golden ale.

My watch read nine o three. There were fourteen hours and fifty-seven minutes of drinking remaining. Gio was excited. Nick was hung over. I was thankful I didn't have to compete.

Their competition grew in importance as other people became aware of it. It never became a widespread campus infatuation along the lines of college football, but those who were in the know began to place bets on which drinker they thought would pull the feat off. There were the obvious bets to place, such as picking the winner. Other side bets included whether you thought both of them would make it to midnight, one would, or neither. There were pools built to bet on the shares of alcohol they would consume during the day. That one didn't fare so well as nearly everyone involved chose beer over hard spirits and wine. These were obscure wagers to reflect their obscure participants. Gio and Nick were not university celebrities, but their face or names were occasionally recognised by the seedy type of folk who also liked to drink too much or place a friendly bet. There were a lot of people like that.

The contest had started out a bit messy. After that first beer, Nick had put on jeans and started on a second. Within the span of the first ten minutes he had already spilled a bit on his jeans. It landed on his crotch. The sort of sophomoric humour that would suggest he might have urinated himself. Vulgar, disgusting, unbelievable: who would enjoy such lowbrow fare?

"Haha, man it looks like you pissed yourself!"

"Yeah, it kind of does. That's hilarious! I'm gonna roll with this."

Nick always had a way of taking the shameful attention and inverting it in to some strange form of empowerment. It was if he wanted others to think that he had pissed his pants. If they thought that, he won. I didn't really understand that. I had come from a long history of shameful attention being nothing more than shameful. Being unable to control a fart during a silent prayer, for example. That's bad enough, but having that happen when seated next to a cute girl you like, that's the worst. It happened. Beet red faces of embarrassment were far more familiar to me than Nick's empowered use of awkwardness. But, as I have mentioned, he just had that ability to dictate the room.

"I'm hungry, let's grab some food, Gio."

With that, Nick in his stained pants, along with Gio and a bewildered version of myself headed down to the cafeteria. After a short breakfast, the competition began in earnest. Nick and Gio kept a steady pace of alcohol going in to their bloodstream. They managed to consume three bottles of beer, each, per hour. It was an alarming amount, but the assuredness of the contestants made the general unease of the rest of us subside. Those of us who had unease, that's. Midge and Whatsherface were cheering loudly for these "pussies" to drink up.

With the drink in them, the boys began to talk. Gio rambled on throughout the day of his many exploits growing up as a military brat, moving from province to province, and then from country to country, going wherever his father was posted. His last several years had been split between Italy and Belgium. In Italy, he had actually gone to school with Whatsherface, a fact that we were not sure Gio even believed. Other seemingly doubtful stories spewed from his mouth when under the influence of "truth serum". He told us about how he had met his girlfriend while high on LSD. He said he had dated Dkembe Mutombo's niece. He had slept with an African president's daughter. A girl had stabbed him with a fork when he broke up with her over dinner. That last one seemed the most unbelievable until he showed us a scar on his abdomen. I forgot to ask him if he still had his appendix.

Nick's drunken stories were far more pedestrian in nature. It was like a drunker version of my own childhood. He and his buddies would stay out late and cause a small ruckus, but usually were harmless to anyone but themselves. His most daring accomplishment in his youth was pissing on an air crash memorial. It was hard to tell whether he meant to be mean spirited or if this was just a youth looking for a place to urinate and he happened to be drinking within twenty feet of a monument. Was he looking for some sort of higher significance? Nick didn't elaborate much on whether this was about some generational battle between reverence and rebellion. I couldn't help but think of my inadvertent vomiting on the side of the campus chapel last night. Was that an intended slight against tradition and hierarchy? I don't remember it that way. I remember in the flash of a second needing a place, any place, to lean against and relieve my stomach. The first place I found coincidentally was the chapel wall. How coincidental was Nick's urination? I'd like to say it didn't have any meaning, but here we were talking about it years later.

Despite the copious, routine amounts of beer entering their systems, Nick and Gio's day actually seemed to fly by in time. In the middle of the afternoon, they took in a football game. In the parking lot before the game, tailgaters barbequed burgers and drank beer behind their vehicles. Nick and Gio wandered among them, snagging a hot dog here and there, stopping to share a beer with new friends. Their advanced inebriation didn't seem out of place in the crowd, helping them to transition from the relative safety of being confined in residence and the dangerous freedom that lurked in the outside world. The game had already started, but many tailgaters lingered in the parking lot well in to the first half. They explained to Nick and Gio that they still had to finish their burgers and beers and then they'd have to let the barbeque cool down and load in to their trucks. Once all that was over then they usually joined the game at the half. New to university life, our contestants listened to the upperclassmen and alumni in the lot. They learned that the football team stunk anyways and that nobody really cared either way. Saturday afternoons meant drinking in a row of trucks outside a half full stadium. Nick and Gio were all too obliged to stick around, sit in some folding camp chairs and shoot the breeze. They found an interesting assortment of people tailgating. All the campus gossip was passed around the crowd. In a small town, with few entertainment options, gossip was currency. The upperclassmen dished out what they had overheard last night at the pub. The alumni shared legendary stories about their favourite professors. In this town everyone had flaws and foibles. Some were earth shattering, others far too ordinary to be noted. Nick and Gio took it all in.

Inside the stadium, the game did end up being a disappointment. The team really did stink and lost the game in the first half. By the time Nick and Gio arrived the game might as well have been over, so deep was the deficit. It didn't matter as the drinking buddies were just looking for a backdrop for their more interesting story; two young men's sauced journey of discovery.

After the game, and back in residence, the homestretch of the contest was appearing on the horizon. Much to my surprise as referee, both men were faring quite well. I was considering devoting my life to studying their superhuman bodies. In order to keep track of their totals, each man had kept their empty bottles, and they confirmed for each other how much each drank at the football game. The number was staggering. At this point both had also kept the same pace. From then until midnight, in order to win someone was going to have to outpace the other.

We gathered in Midge's room and got in to our normal routine of picking apart her sentences. Regional expressions were always up for discussion as our group came from across the country and what we had always assumed were normal phrases where we came from were unheard of in other regions, or were a different variant. Nick's Maritime expressions, no matter how ridiculous they sounded, always seemed to win new admirers. I believe he had me sold that an exaggerated fall was actually falling "ass over tea kettle". You can't argue with a nice turn of phrase like that. It was beautifully, elegantly constructed and delivered with just the right amount of folksy elocution to impress any ear. Midge, on the other hand, was from Southern Ontario and suffered from the same linguistic disabilities many residents of that region do. Precision was always lacking, for one. Telling us one of her friends was going to the University of Western Ontario in London had the rest of us checking our maps to see if that was a satellite campus. Apparently the western part of the province was in the southeast. She tried to explain it to me, but it never got past the part of me asking which province is west of Ontario. As soon as we can all agree that Manitoba is on the western frontier of Ontario, the sooner we can agree that the University of Western Ontario needs to be moved to Thunder Bay or Kenora. Misuse of real words was another. When we bothered her, she asked us to stop harping her. That seemed like a perfectly nice thing to do. Angels played harps. We were being angelic, you might say. It was all the more fun to note that she was a modern languages major. There was some hope that English might be included in her requisite studies.

The night passed quickly and those of us who had started drinking in the evening were still feeling pretty good. Nick and Gio, however, were finally appearing human. Neither one looked particularly healthy, either. Nick left to get another beer from his fridge and didn't return. We went to check on him and he had fallen asleep on his bed, fully clothed. This was at eleven thirty two. He had only needed to go another twenty-eight minutes to finish. In the meantime, Gio continued to drink and in that final stretch to midnight drank an additional two beers on top of what Nick had. At the stroke of midnight I officially declared him the winner, which was unnecessary, as Nick had lost the moment he passed out. Gio, I think, just wanted to complete the marathon for good measure. By my count Gio had drank forty-five beers in fifteen hours. Nick, not to be discounted, had still managed to drink forty-three in fourteen and a half hours. What we had was a Mark McGuire Sammy Sosa showdown of beer, both to be commended for their efforts.

It was the next day, around noon and I was sitting in Midge's room, watching a movie, when Gio popped in to say hello. He was wearing the clothes from last night and had a beer in hand.

"What's up?"

"Just watching a movie."

"Dude, I just woke up and there was a beer next to my bed."

"Was not it warm?"

"Yeah, man."

It was really hard not to see how that might bother any other person. Gio, champion of the drinking world, however, had no such boundaries.

"So, you are drinking a warm beer?"

"Yeah, man."

Later in the afternoon, Nick finally joined us. He looked like shit and smelled almost as bad. What had happened to him was clear. This was a man who had drank forty-three beers and then passed out. It took all the glamour away from the accomplishments of yesterday. It was a behind the scenes look at something no one had ever really wanted to see. Drunkards were cool in university, and to see someone match the feats of Animal House brought part of the whole experience to a deeper level of awesomeness. But no one had any interest in witnessing the most gruesome form of hangover you could imagine. Plus, the smell was truly dreadful. Nick's body odour permeated from his skin to the clothes he wore and finally, without any real delay, found itself travelling deep within our noses.

"You look and smell like shit."

"Thanks, Midge. I hadn't noticed."

"Really? We could smell you coming down the hallway."

"That was sarcastic, you stupid bitch."

"Oh, Nick. You are pretty hung over."

Got to hand it to Nick, even when he was being incredibly offensive and was physically nauseating to be near, somehow, in even these moments, he had a way of charming everyone. He really did look and smell like shit, though. Gio, however, looked, smelled, and sounded as if nothing had happened the day before.

"Aren't you hung over, Gio?"

"Yeah, man."

"You really don't look it."

"Oh."

Nick was flummoxed. He really couldn't comprehend how Gio might have been able to outlast him and then appear perfectly fine the next day. He did, however, begin to formulate his own defence. Men, you may already know, are creatures driven by ego.

"It's pretty crazy, Nick, that Gio just woke up, beer in hand and kept going today."

"I think I have probably had three or four since I woke up."

"Nice, that must be a great two day tally. Forty-eight or nine, is it?"

"Wait a second, before Gio goes on about his two day total, may I remind you of Friday night?"

It's funny how long ago Friday night had felt. I had forgotten where I put the phone number that woman outside Klub Karaoke had given me. It was on a receipt somewhere. I usually throw out receipts, so it was probably lost now.

"What about Friday?"

"Jonathan will vouch for me on this one, we had twelve beer each before we went to Klub Karaoke. I drank two pitchers to myself there, while he was outside making out with some dirty older woman. And when we got back to rez, I drank two bottles before I crashed."

No wonder Nick had looked so awful the morning of the contest, he was hung over from having drank the equivalent of twenty two beers the night before.

"He did drink all that."

"Wait, Nick, are you saying that you think you were more impressive?"

Women needed to learn the ego thing very early in adult life to understand most of our behaviour. Midge was not quite there yet, but was working on it.

"Well, Midge, if everybody is impressed that Gio woke up today and drank a beer, and his two day total is forty eight or nine, I'd just like to point out that with yesterday and Friday I ended up with a two day total of sixty-five beer. That's all I want to say."

A compromise was agreed upon at that point to spare the egos of the two valiant, and ultimately stupid competitors. Gio would forever be known as the one day champion of drinking, having consumed forty-five beers on a Saturday that September. After adding to his tally on the Sunday, Nick laid claim to an impressive weekend total of seventy four beers, a mark that as far as any of us know, stands to this day among eighteen-year-old university freshmen.'"

Jonathan wondered if any of his graduating classmates even remembered that story. It was just four years ago, but he remembered it as being the time when anything was possible. Now only one possibility sat in front of them all.

Ten

Jonathan leaned against the bar, waiting for any of the dozen bartenders to notice the twenty dollar bill in his hand. He was out with some friends and all of them were dancing and laughing on the dance floor. Jonathan just wanted another beer.

-What can I get you?

-I'll have a Kokanee.

-Great, Kokanee.

The bartender disappeared around the corner of the bar to the other side where the Kokanee tap was located. It was in that split second that about three other bartenders asked Jonathan if they could get him a drink. It was just like waiting for a bus. When you want a bus you stand by the side of the road for what seems like ages until one comes along, and then, it usually comes along with all the other routes. It's what makes changing buses nearly impossible. Jonathan was always just missing the bus he really wanted. Why couldn't they find a better stagger system? He thought the bartenders could use a similar arrangement. If there was one thing they ought to borrow from buses, Jonathan thought, it would be a pull cord to let everyone know that you need to get off. This drinking was dangerous business.

-$7.50, please.

Jonathan handed over the twenty and waited again while the bartender disappeared around the corner to get change. A couple more bartenders came by to ask if anyone needed a drink. Jonathan just smiled as he took a sip from the pint glass. Looking around there were a lot of good-looking women. He saw his friends on the dance floor talking up some cuties and went to go join them.

-Hi!

-Hi!

-Great music, eh?!

-Yeah!

-It's good to dance to!

-Yeah!

Jonathan was not really doing himself any favours. His drink had been spilling everywhere as his body bounced, almost with the beat of the loud music pounding through their eardrums.

-Do you like to dance?!

-I'm dancing!

-I know! I meant in general!

-Where?!

-In general!

-I don't think I have been to that place!

-It's not a club!

-What?!

-I said it's not a club!

-What?! I can't hear you!

-I can't yell any louder!

-Louder?!

-Yeah! I can't yell any louder!

-What?!

-Nevermind.

Jonathan weaved his way through the crowd, losing more of his beer in the process, until he was safely at the edge of the dance floor. There were no tables to sit at as they were filled with groups of friends sitting around chatting or couples making out. Jonathan watched one of the couples exchange saliva. It was captivating like a car crash, he knew.

-Hey Jon, man, how are ya?

-Oh, hey, I'm good, you?

It was a friend of a friend of Jonathan's, barely an acquaintance.

-I'm good, I'm good.

-Nice.

-There is a lot of fine tail here tonight.

-Yeah, that's right.

-Too bad for you, you are rocking the mo.

-Heh? Oh, right, the mustache.

Yeah man, you guys are making it too easy for the rest of us.

-You are a smooth faced bastard; you know that?

-I do know that. And so will that girl over there.

Jonathan was good to be rid of the jerk. He was exactly the kind of superficial jerk that Jonathan despised. There ought to be a place where people like that could go to get away from people like me, Jonathan thought.

The music was thumping in a steady carnal beat and bodies were grinding against each other making the fabric between them feel embarrassed. Jonathan could only let his imagination run wild as beautiful women passed him by. Average women who were looking their best also passed by, and they found a spot in Jonathan's imagination, too. Finally, less than attractive women were given some of Jonathan's attention as his mood plummeted and expectations and standards with them. Jonathan joined the dance floor and flung his body against anyone and anything with a mad intent. His friends nearby only cheered him on.

-Go Jon, go!

-You the man, Jon!

-Yeah!

-Ladies, he's single!

-He gives the best mustache rides!

Jonathan found himself wedged between his dance partner and the back of another man who was dancing with his own girl. The other man was violently encroaching on Jonathan's space and he had nowhere else to go. Hoping to diffuse the situation, Jonathan wrapped his arms around his dance partner and pulled himself closer to her.

-What are you doing?!

-I thought we were dancing!

-I have a boyfriend!

-What?!

-I have a boyfriend! He's just over there!

-I didn't know!

Jonathan looked across the floor at a tall, muscular looking guy. He had a military build and the dumb haircut to match.

-Fuck.

-It's okay! Just stop touching me!

-I'm sorry! This guy behind me keeps pushing me!

-Are you kidding?!

-No!

-Well push back!

Jonathan was not about to push anyone. He also was aware he was just wasting his time with this woman while her boyfriend was twenty feet away.

-I've gotta go to the washroom!

-Alright!

Jonathan slid his way off the dance floor and slowly began making his way to the washroom. It was all the way at the other end of the bar and downstairs. Along the way he witnessed a parade of comedies in each booth.

-No, I wasn't looking at that girl!

-You looked, Tony!

-I didn't look! Fuck, what do you want me to say?

-Don't swear at me, you fuckface!

-That's enough, please. I swear I didn't look at anyone.

-Shots! Who wants them some shots?!

-Yeah, yeah! Right here! You the man!

-What are we drinking?

-It's called a blowjob.

-That's wild, man, wild.

-Bottoms up!

-So I says to son, I says, listen man, you need to step back or I'm about to make you step back.

-What he do?

-The punk didn't do n'thing.

-So what you do?

-I clocked him upside the head.

-Dude, I can't believe we got in!

-Quiet, don't look so obvious.

-Shit, I think I see one of my teachers.

-That guy? Sorry Ronnie, I think I might have grinded with him a bit.

-You grinded with my teacher? Gross!

-Just a bit.

Jonathan reached the stairwell and started to descend his way down. Along the way other people started passing him, obviously in more of a rush to piss or snort blow. It was not made any easier by the volume of people trying to go up the stairs and return to the bar. Jonathan was stuck in the middle of the stairs for what seemed like ages. He'd move faster but his legs felt wobbly and he didn't really feel like ending up on his face at the bottom.

-C'mon man, move along.

-I am, I am.

-You alright, man?

-I'm fine. I just need to piss.

At the bottom, Jonathan turned the corner and found himself facing two lineups. In the ladies' line he saw a continuous row of hotties, each more lovely than the last. In the men's line he saw a continuous row of assholes, each more of a douche than the last. They were all probably at the bar together. What the hell, Jonathan wondered, why would anyone want to be with these guys? Jonathan figured that he was ten times the man any of these guys could be.

-Hey.

-Seriously? You are going to try and hit on me in a bathroom line?

-Maybe?

-Fuck off, creep.

Lesbian, Jonathan thought.

Wait, did you really think that, Jonathan? Did you think that because a woman rejects you she is not sexually attracted to anyone of your gender? Are you that stupid?

-No, I didn't really believe that at all.

Why did you think it?

-It was a way to dismiss rejection. I'm insecure.

Well, if it's not too much trouble, I'd really like you to man up. I'm beginning to lose interest in you as the protagonist of my book.

-Now you know how I feel.

Is there anyway we can course correct this evening?

-No, I'm fairly certain it's a lost cause tonight.

Jonathan went upstairs and left the bar. He flagged down a cab and returned home to bed. He woke up in his bar clothes lying on his couch. Next to him laid his notebook. In barely legible printing was something he had apparently written when he got home.

Skirt Season

"There is an amazing phenomenon that happens twice a school year. In a harsh winter climate like in small town Quebec, much of the school year is dominated by sensible clothing, built for warmth and comfort. Sweatpants, sweaters, parkas, toques, and longjohns find themselves as the default fashion. However, at the very beginning of the school year, as the sticky humid summer winds down, and at the very end of the school year, as a warm spring appears, there is skirt weather.

Nick and I were sitting in the cafeteria; it must have been about the second week of school and one of the resident assistants from our building asked if he could join us. We had met him before and found him to be a pretty decent guy when off duty and agreed.

"So, how you guys liking it so far?"

"It's pretty good. I like it here."

"Yeah, classes seem interesting. Lots of cool people."

"And the girls? You guys seen some of the bodies on these girls?"

What a second line to say to two complete strangers. I was in awe of his frankness, but Nick didn't seem fussed about it.

"Tell me about it. There is nothing like this back home. I mean there obviously were great looking girls, but just not so many all in one place."

"And the skirts!"

"Yeah, man, I'm really digging the skirts."

"Well, I have to tell you guys this, because this is your first year and you haven't experienced anything like this before; almost all of these girls are going to gain weight this year."

"What?"

"It's a beautiful thing, boys, don't worry about it. It's called the freshman fifteen and everyone puts it on. It may not be exactly fifteen, but everyone gains a little weight in first year."

"Really?"

"Oh, yeah, and the beautiful thing about all these attractive women is that they will be surprised by it."

"That's beautiful?"

"Yeah, it is, man. Listen, right now all these hotties are walking around in tight t-shirts and those skirts, damn those skirts, and everyone is checking them out and they are used to that. They've been practicing for this moment all summer back home. They are stuck-up, they know they are hot, and they have great expectations about what that can get you in life. But, as soon as that cool air starts to come flowing in to town, and people get used to the slow pace of university life, they and their fashion choices start to relax. Loose, warm clothing is de rigueur. They discover beer, poutine, taking naps instead of heading to the gym. Ugg boots replace high heels. It happens. Four or five months of this happens. And everyone, I mean everyone, you guys included, are blissfully unaware. You will find some girl at the bar and she'll be wearing loose fitting clothes and you will take her home and won't notice she's got a few extra curves. You are just thrilled to have her come home. It's okay, it's natural, man. She won't know any different either. This is a beautiful, strange time in all our lives. But, and this is the truly amazing phenomenon that happens, come April, when the weather turns nice, the skirts and those tight t-shirts return. Only this time, instead of fitting just right, they are way too tight to fit properly around those extra pounds. And these girls don't have any other spring or summer clothes with them here. So, for a few weeks, this campus is littered with tight, ill-fitting clothing on all the freshmen girls. It's natural, man, and I love it. You get to really see everything pop out, and a love handle, here or there, is nothing to shy away from. The amazing thing is that girls that have no curves right now, all of a sudden, it appears to you, will have boobs and butts that you want to get with, and a lot of those stuck up girls that wouldn't give you the time of day now, might consider it then. They are all self-conscious and it means that a fellow who does not mind holding on to a bit more will find himself getting pretty lucky then. Also, I have heard that sex is a great relief from exam stress. I don't know if it is or not, but I have definitely used that line before and had it work. Remember I told you this in the spring and buy me a beer when it happens, boys."

Nick and I were dumbfounded with this information. Every beautiful girl who walked by in tight t-shirts and short skirts became increasingly beautiful with the sad belief that she might lose some of that lustre in less than eight months. I wanted to tell them not to get that second slice of pizza from the cafeteria, but I was not really any better prepared. I ate tons of poutine. I drank tons of beer. I learned that a nap between classes was more enjoyable than a trip to the gym. As I worried about those girls adding on pounds, I simultaneously put on my own. Luckily I didn't have to wear a skirt in April.

That spring, and every spring after that I was at university I always loved sitting in the quad, watching the girls walk to the library to study for exams, letting a little bit of extra skin pop out from between their tight tees and that short skirt. Their bums seemed to have a little bit more of a wiggle to them, their boobs seemed a bit too round, and the whole package made all of those girls seem way more real than the cookie cutter dolls that arrived every fall, fresh from high school. It really was a beautiful phenomenon.'"

Eleven

Jonathan sat there in his bar clothes and could only shake his head.

-What the hell was that all about?

He examined the state of his clothes and saw stains all over them and could smell the stench of stale beer on him.

-Fucking pathetic.

There was no excuse he could think of to justify living like this. It was a sad, sorry existence for someone so young and still full of potential.

-What am I doing?

He couldn't come up with an answer. Jonathan sat in empty contemplation for nearly an hour. He had no idea which direction he was going, but he was fairly certain it was not forward. He was ashamed of his behaviour at the bar. It was not all just having a good time. There was a desperate plea Jonathan was crying out that he needed meaning and purpose. What was the point of grinding on a stranger? It was so primal, so base, so pointless. His looking at women had moved far beyond the acknowledgement of beauty to festering a deep desire to fuck the brains out of every last one of them. Even if that were true in the darkest cellars of Jonathan's mind, it was not a particularly pleasing thought. He thought of his professor and the vending machine. How wrong that must be, Jonathan thought, surely there was meant to be something special about two bodies coming together. It was not a mechanistic connection like refuelling a plane in the air. They have heartbeats! You can feel the other person's beat intensify and quicken its pace. That surely has to have meaning! Jonathan wanted to know that it was true. He wanted to know that there was something more going on than biology. He needed to know that this was far more complex than the instructions to assemble a bookshelf. That was why this was so frustrating. Life does not come with an instruction manual. Jonathan realised life does not even come to an agreed upon end. Forget trying to argue about how we get there, Jonathan didn't know where there was.

"I stared out in to the blankness of everything and realized with the utmost certainty that all of this was meaningless. The drink, the drugs, the sex, the violence. Every action was without intent. We were accidentally working our way towards adulthood. There was no rudder to steer us. That didn't matter without a compass and an idea for a destination, both of which we were also missing. I had to stop and ask myself one fundamental question. No, it was not "who am I?" as profound as we often wish to make that one; it is in fact fairly obvious. The question I had to stop and ask was "who do I want to be?" It's not this, which was clear. No man wakes up and decides

to be an underachieving slob. Things happen, horribly tiny things, things that you don't even notice until it's too late and then you are everything you never thought you would be. What do you do then? I knew it came down to making life-altering decisions. That sounds ominous and I will admit I didn't mean for it to carry such dramatic weight, but it is, in its way, ominous. The difference between drifting along aimlessly and being in control of your destiny was as simple as standing up and saying "I'm here". No man can truly take account for his life until he first admits that he exists. We try to hide that, I think, when life just sort of happens. It's easy then to play the victim and question what happens to us, but ultimately we're in control not of what the world does to us, but what we can do to the world. It sounds as if we're given a great amount of power, and in a way we are. It's not physical, financial, political or religious power. There are no buildings dedicated to your power. It's in your mind. Each one of us has the capacity to move forward and live the kinds of lives we want. It can be an empty superficial life, drifting without meaning. Or, better still, it can be a life worth remembering, one filled with meaning. The big thing to know is that things are at their very core meaningless. Only we can give and take away meaning. It's a powerful thing, but it's also vulnerable. As soon as you give a person, place or thing meaning, anyone else has the ability to desecrate it and dishonour your meaning. Mecca is just a city until someone gives it meaning."

"Jon, you are so fucking high right now."

"No, Charlie, I have never been so clear. It all makes so much sense."

"But what happens when we give meaning to things that should be meaningless? Maybe Mecca should just be a city."

"Yeah, I know. That's the powerful thing, man, is that nothing has any meaning until we give it meaning."

"Exactly, but it's dangerous."

"Gio is right. This is the cause of every single conflict. People don't fight meaningless wars."

"Sure they do, there are tons of examples."

"Not of meaningless wars. Every war has rightly or wrongly been given some meaning by those in power and the people have accepted that."

"Look at Vietnam, that objectively had no real meaning to the U.S. until they believed that it did."

"There were thousands of men who went to fight in Vietnam without any understanding of how a civil war in an Asian country mattered to them."

"It was about stopping the spread of communism."

"Bullshit."

"It was."

"That's what was said."

"Communism continued to spread in the 1970s and 80s, regardless of the U.S. going to Vietnam. If anything, their withdrawal, that defeat that they won't admit, fuelled the spread of communist thoughts. It was strong enough to put off the mighty USA so maybe it's right for us."

"But not strong enough to defeat Islam."

"Right, that's right. The Soviets couldn't beat the Mujahaddin in Afghanistan."

"And look where that's taken us."

"Right, that's right, man. The idea of a militaristic Islam is fuelled by this transit of properties: Islam can beat communism which beat capitalism, therefore Islam can beat capitalism."

"But that's wrong, too. We know that. It's not about Islam versus capitalism. Look at Dubai and Abu Dhabi. There are tons of other examples, too. The point is that they like capitalism. They like making money. That's not the battle of ideas they are looking for."

"It's about anti-power, wherever they are, whatever form of power is trying to push down on them. Nobody likes to be on the bottom."

"Yeah, yeah, man, that makes a lot of sense."

"Capitalism is liked when you are part of the winners, it's despised when you are not."

"It's not about Islam, then, at all."

"No, not really. Not when you have Muslims in the Gulf making billions off of land they accidentally discovered oil in. That's when they become winners."

"It's the losers, the ones that need to rely on outsiders for handouts or help that get upset when those handouts come with conditions."

"You could argue that those lands in the Gulf were handouts. The way that region was carved up by imaginary boundaries."

"That's right. Those places only became places because they said they were."

"They gave meaning to nothing."

"It was all a bunch of sand, before."

"Not quite, but yeah."

"There were people there, before."

"Sure, but those people didn't have any meaning until it was decided they did."

"Can we do that?"

"It's been done."

"Interesting."

"They are all strangers anyways. They don't mean anything to me. That is, they don't mean anything to me until I consider them like me."

"They are like you."

"They are like me."

"And, once someone becomes like you, violence is impossible."

"It's impossible."

"How could anyone wish violence against themselves?"

"That's self-abuse."

"We put those people on suicide watch."

"They are trying to kill themselves. It's unhealthy."

"Right, exactly."

"That's why I'm a pacifist."

"You are a pacifist?"

"For sure, it's a simple thing. All you have to do is ask yourself if you'd want to be killed and if you would want to kill."

"Logical."

"Unfortunately we aren't logical creatures, are we?"

"No, I think we like to pretend that we are."

"That's how you can create false meaning."

"False meaning?"

"Pretend."

"Ah, right. Pretend meaning."

"We're so high."

"Very, extremely high."

"That does not make any of this less true."

"No, but it makes it difficult to remember tomorrow."

"True."

"Yes, it's true."

"It's all true."

"It's true because we all agree it's true."

"You just fucked my mind, dude."

"Very true."

"But what are we supposed to do with this if we don't remember tomorrow?"

"We will get high again."

"That's a solution."

"Is it?"

"Yes, if we forget what we talked about tonight tomorrow, we will retrace our footsteps."

"That's what you do when you are lost."

"Correct, when you are lost, you retrace your footsteps."

"But that just takes us back."

"Right, we want to go back."

"Not all the way back."

"No, I suppose not."

"So we want to retrace our footsteps back to the point where we agreed we all need to move forward."

"Yes, that's right, we need to go back to the place to go forward."

"When will we do that?"

"Tomorrow, when we need to remember what we did today."

"It will be yesterday tomorrow."

"Tomorrow we will remember yesterday, which is today, what we agreed upon on what needs to be done to move forward tomorrow, which will be today tomorrow."

"But, what does it all mean?"

"It means what we say it means."

"What happens when others say it means something different?"

"What happens when their meaning is different?"

"Different and combative?"

"Ideas cannot fight."

"No, but people will fight on their behalf."

"I won't."

"No?"

"No, remember I'm a pacifist."

"Right."

"Yes, I remember. We should all be pacifists."

"We should."

"What happens when someone else does not agree with us?"

"Shit."

"How did we get here?"

"Let's retrace our steps."

"We're all so lost."

Five years later and Jonathan was telling the same story. It's funny how everything has been done before. It's funny how history is filled with the same mistakes repeated over and over again. Really, it's quite funny. This is a comedy, remember?

Twelve

-Morning Jonathan, how are you?

-Good, good, thanks. How are you?

-I'm good. Did you have a good weekend?

-Yeah, it was pretty good.

-What did you get up to?

-Oh, not too much. Same old, same old. You?

-Yeah, mostly the same. We went to this great restaurant on Saturday, an Italian place, I will have to give you the address, I highly recommend it.

-Great, thanks. I'm always looking for somewhere new.

-They made the best fettuccini I have ever had.

-Wow, really? You better let me know where this place is. I like Italian.

-Sure, I will let you know.

-Great, thanks. Have a good day.

-You too, Jonathan.

Jonathan sat down at his workstation and turned on the computer. The obsolete machine took forever to start up. In the meantime, Jonathan changed out of his sneakers in to his dress shoes. He felt like Mister Rogers having indoor and outdoor shoes. The only thing he was missing was a change of cardigan.

-Hey Jonathan, how was your weekend?

-It was okay, you?

-Oh man, did you see the game on Saturday? It was unreal.

-Oh did you go, Philippe?

-No, I didn't, but watching it on TV gave me goose bumps.

-Wow, that good, eh?

-Did you not see it?

-No, I missed it. To be honest I don't even know the score.

-What?! Are you kidding me? You didn't watch?

-No.

-It was the best game of the year. It might even be the best game I have ever watched.

-Really?

-Well, maybe not the best, I remember in '93, but this was pretty close.

-Wow that's quite a statement.

-I think this is the year.

-It's still way too early to say that.

-You didn't see the game. I'm telling you this is the year. They look so good. You really need to believe me.

-You are right, I didn't see the game, but there is still two thirds of the regular season to play. Slumps happen. Not to mention that the playoffs still have to happen. Anything can happen then.

-Jonathan, you just need to watch them play.

-I watched them play last week!

-Yeah, but you missed Saturday. Saturday they were on another planet.

-Sometimes I think you are on a different planet, Philippe.

-If it's the same planet as them, I'd be okay with that.

-Who knows, maybe I'm the one on a different planet.

-Oh yeah?

-Yeah, it seems like sometimes I'm just drifting in and out and everyone else is doing their own thing. Sometimes I'm in sync, and other times not so much.

-Have you had a coffee yet?

-No.

-You want to go?

-Sure, why not.

-Just let me go drop off my stuff at my desk.

-Okay.

Jonathan took the opportunity to check the box score for Saturday's game. Philippe was correct in describing a commanding performance, but Jonathan was steadfast in his belief that you can't determine the champion this early. The best he thought most people could do was name a handful of teams that had a good shot. Usually everyone agreed on the same handful. That was the best prognostication to expect.

-Ready to go?

-Yeah, I'm, let's go.

-So what did you get up to this weekend?

-Oh, not too much, just the same as always.

-Right on.

-Did you visit your girlfriend?

-Yeah, I did.

-How is she?

-Oh she is the best; she watched the game with me. Just the best.

-Haha, I meant more in general, how is she doing?

-Ah, I see. She is doing well.

-That's good.

-How about you? Any ladies?

-Not at the moment, no.

-Why not? You are a good looking guy. If you don't mind me saying. I'm not gay or anything.

-Yeah, I know. You were just talking about your girlfriend.

-Right. I just meant it's a bit odd for another guy to compliment on looks.

-I don't think so. I don't find that odd.

-You don't? I mean it's a bit unusual, but I just wanted to give you a boost of confidence. I mean, with that mustache, you could be a young Tom Selleck.

-Haha, thanks. That's the idea.

-Have you raised a lot of money?

-A bit, yeah. It's hard though when everyone else is doing the same thing.

-I don't think I could do it. Do you think I would look strange with a mustache?

-Are you asking me to comment on your looks now, Philippe?

-Oh, right. I just meant I have never been able to wear a mustache. Even my beard is just something that comes from a lazy few days. I don't let it get out of control. I don't know if it would look right at work. People might, uh, give me odd looks. Do people give you odd looks, Jonathan?

-I don't know. They kind of just give me the same look they always do.

-Maybe it's because a mustache suits you.

-People have said that. I don't know what that means.

-I mean, it just looks like you could have a mustache.

-I do have a mustache.

-No, but I mean for real.

-This is real.

-You know what I meant.

-Yes, I did, but I like to be facetious, it's when I'm at my best.

-Facetious? I don't know that word. What does it mean?

-Oh, it sort of means that I was being serious but in a silly way.

-Like sarcasm?

-No, not really. A bit. I don't think I explained it well. It's just being facetious, I guess.

-It sounds like, uh, feces. You know?

-Yeah, I hear that. In a way you could say that I was being shitty, I guess.

-Would you say that?

-Not in polite company.

-I'm not polite?

-You are very polite, Philippe. It's another English expression. It means like in more formal situations.

-You are wearing a tie, Jonathan, how more formal can we get?

-Hmm, let's see if I can explain this better. You and I are friends, wouldn't you agree?

-Yes, sure.

-So in friendly situations, like between you and I, we speak in more familiar terms.

-Oh okay, like in, uh, French, we use the tu form?

-Yes, perfect. It's exactly like that. You use tu when you talk to someone you are familiar with, your friends, your family, and people like that.

-Right, and we use vous when we talk to our boss or our elders, or people we don't know.

-Exactly. What's that called again?

-It's the politesse.

-Now where do you think the English got the word polite from?

-Oh! Very clever.

-So I should not use words like shitty around my boss or elderly people, or complete strangers.

-No, but I wouldn't recommend using it around anyone. It's not a very good word.

-It's not polite.

-No, it's not polite. Also, it's just a really lazy word that people insert instead of actually describing. How was your dinner last night? Oh, it was shitty.

-Not a good image.

-No, the last thing I want to do is imagine feces all over my food.

-Do you eat fast food?

Jonathan burst in to laughter. Philippe was still working on his English; he had a strong command of the language though he still needed to figure out the nuances, but damn, if he didn't have great timing on jokes.

-Brilliant.

The two men stood in line at the coffee shop and joked further about small differences in understanding that inevitably come up when one was speaking their second language.

Back at his workstation, Jonathan began his day with earnest. Opening up the word processor and typing up a short note his boss had requested.

-Hey Jon.

-Morning, Michel.

-Did you want to go for coffee?

-I've already gone, thanks. I just got back.

-No worries.

The day continued along like that. It always seemed to.

-Hey, you are no help.

I'm sorry, Jonathan, but I have got to place you in a believable world of ennui. The least you can do is put up with it for the sake of me telling my story.

-But I don't want you to tell your story. You are going to make me look like a pathetic fool.

Aren't you?

-Yes, but that's not the point.

Well, what's the point?

-The point, if there has to be one, is that through the magic of words we can create our own fantasies. We can escape the doldrums of the cold modern world. Yes, I know that I sit in an endless sea of sky blue cubicles. But wouldn't I rather be outside, flying through the blue sky? I could be a superhero. This could be my cover.

You are not a superhero, Jonathan. You are my protagonist. I like you.

-You have a funny way of showing it.

What would be the fun in lavishing you with riches? Do you think anyone would want to read about that? It's not you, man. It's not.

-You didn't have to make me balding.

No, but people like flaws they can relate to.

-So, what am I supposed to do? Give me some instruction. Anything, please.

I thought you were on a journey of self-discovery. I'm just trying to facilitate it. I don't want to force anything. I have never enjoyed the use of deus ex machina in stories. It's ham-fisted. I think we're both better than that, Jonathan.

-Do you want me to keep sitting here at this workstation?

Would it be believable for you, as a character, to leave in the middle of the day from work?

-No, I suppose not. Unless I was sick.

Jonathan is not sick.

-You think you are pretty fucking clever, don't you?

A little, yes. But, I will try to take it easier on you. I will skip the story ahead to when you get home from work. You can take it from there.

-You are a bit of a control freak.

I thought I was being relatively benign. Light touches here and there, that sort of thing. You are the one who is trying to author a novel for your generation.

-I think people will relate.

The title might grab their attention, but it's a bit much, don't you think?

-'Funeral for the Young'?

Yeah, people will think it's about fourteen year old meth addicts joining suicide pacts.

-You think?

I don't know. It just seems far scarier than the banal collection of university rememberings of an office worker. I think readers would go in to it expecting to be shocked with ritualistic cults and the like. Your story might bore them.

-Crazy things happen.

Yeah, sure. But are they really all that unique?

-They felt unique at the time.

How many books, television shows, and movies have you witnessed describe the exact same type of events?

-Lots.

That's right. It's all been done before.

-But I want to tell my story. My story has value!

Does it?

-It does, I swear it does. It may not be new, but I can tell it in a new way.

Well, go ahead. You are in that place.

Jonathan sat at his desk and began to type.

Upside Down Week

"It was a tradition that started in second semester and continued throughout our university careers. In the middle of every semester, usually when we had midterms or papers approaching, Nick, Gio and myself would go nocturnal. It usually worked without much fuss. I tended to only take classes early in the day and then evening courses. That allowed me the opportunity to go to sleep in the afternoon. Essentially my courses were inversed to match my body. My evening courses were now the first thing I saw in a day and my morning classes were the last. In the interim, the three of us would gather at night and talk philosophy, drink black coffee, and work on our papers or study. It was damned quiet during the middle of the night. There was a reassuring peace about it. Lost in the hustle of student life was the realisation that things can slow down, that we really can control the pace of our lives, that there might be a way to appreciate our time and our place on this planet. I loved upside down week because it added meaning. It was ours and it was special. We knew lots of people who pulled all nighters, and we were among those people ourselves, but that was not the same. An allnighter was fraught with stress, a need for speed, a pressure to deliver something at the end. If someone stayed up all night writing with the intention of having a finished essay what chance would they have to slow down and smell the proverbial roses? We

101

were not trying to do that. Upside down week, as much as it was about flipping our schedules around for the sole purpose of being different, was also a quasi-spiritualistic journey. It was our peyote walk through the desert. Minus the peyote, walking and desert. It was in these quiet hours when Nick or Gio would reveal far more about themselves than they would ever let on during the daylight. You can truly learn about a friend by sharing silence comfortably. Not that awkward silence where both parties feel that there ought to be words, but a comfortable silence that just is.

In our second and third years, when we lived in a house together, Nick arranged his rather large bedroom like a living room and it became the headquarters for late night philosophy sessions and by extension, the home of upside down week when it rolled around. In his room, Nick had moved two futons around a coffee table and put his bed at the back of the room, out of the way. It almost became the last refuge of the house, as it became the only clean room left. Living with four guys had not produced the tidiest home and efforts to regulate it had left it running amok. As a terrifying parallel to our planet's own devastation, it really did seem like rather than clean up the boys were content to destroy everything in their path and continue on to cleaner rooms before they too would become scorched earth. Nick's room was the last refuge and the boys gathered there in the middle of the night, presumably after waging war and destruction elsewhere during the day. It was in these moments that we would enter in to, without intended irony, philosophical debates about the purpose of life. I had argued that the true purpose of life was to create, in whatever form. The way that the boys had created a mess was not really what I meant. They could also learn to create clean dishes. They could create a healthy living environment. They could create reasonably responsible hygiene habits. They could create relief for the long-suffering roommate. Ah, philosophy is filled with wonderful hypothetical situations. I was not interested in trying to use the Socratic method to try asking them about the good life and emptying garbage bins. There were only so many ways to try to influence behaviour and this was not it. Unfortunately, in this case, leading by example, while a morally superior method, was also ineffectual. If you want to get others to do dishes as soon as they are done with them, then you, too, must wash dishes immediately. If, like myself, you prefer to wash dishes once a day, to include the bowl and spoon from breakfast, the small plate and fork from lunch, the large plate, fork, knife, pan, and spatula from dinner, along with likely one or two glasses and a coffee mug, with small spoon, then you will find that it becomes impossible to change the behaviour of others. If they see you leave behind that plate and fork, then they, too, will leave behind their plate and fork. Your intention of washing it later may not be in their mind at all. Perhaps they have no intention of washing it ever because they saw you appear to have no intention of washing now. Or, perhaps, they do have the intention of washing it later, but their idea of later is much longer over the horizon than you might imagine. A horrible habit of the boys was to leave a sink of dirty dishes in perpetual existence. They would grab new dishes from the cupboards until the cupboards were bare and then they would reach in to that dirty sink and wash exactly what they needed for their meal. When they were finished, they would then return the used dish to the sink, possibly for safe storage. That pile could sit in the sink up to six weeks before the pressure would get to me and I'd have to wash every last dish, letting them air dry on tea towels spread across every flat surface I could find in the kitchen. The table, counters, and stovetop would all be used. The whole vicious cycle would begin again the moment someone grabs a bowl resting on the table, and return it to the sink after cereal. It didn't even have a chance to end up in the cupboard. That was the problem with doing a large load of dishes, it didn't have to be six weeks worth, but even doing my day's use of dishes, there would be free riders. One fork, Jon, just one fork, it's all I used. You wouldn't mind, cheers. Jon, you are already doing all these, you mind if I toss in this plate, thanks. What a bunch of clueless dicks.

Aside from the domestic issues, there was always a reason to enjoy our time together as roommates and upside down week was the epitome of our friendships. We could get drawn in to intense debates that only people who truly can appreciate debate – the juggling of ideas in a masturbatory display of intelligence – would want to be around. There are many people I know who are extremely intelligent but cannot enjoy the back and forth of a solid debate. For women, especially, there is often an unease to even witnessing the jostling of two young bucks, butting heads over ideas. I'd like to apologise, but for most of us, young educated men in the twenty first century, there are not really too many options to show our capacity, and by extension, our worth. In older times, it may have been perfectly acceptable to beat your opponent with a blunt object, but that's assault, brother, we've got laws against that now. Heck, we've got laws. That alone shows that we're beyond the point of when demonstrating our own superiority could ever be done using violent force. Sure, sports can do that, in their own way, demonstrating the physical attributes of athletes, but that's hardly the only way to show who we're. For most of us, young scholars, our best athletic days passed us by long ago, if ever. But in the use of our minds, in our minds we're just getting started. I don't know if we ever fully talked the idea through, but if we're to believe anything about progress (and there are doubts) and the evolution of man, whether on a macro, micro, or meso scale, we need to also consider within one man. There has got to be a drive within us to move beyond our caveman like behaviour in our youth (though I realise that this story so far has demonstrated the opposite). At the point that we metaphorically stand on our hind legs and begin to think, it's time to think seriously. The natural progression, if possible, has to be to think deeply and with meaning on subjects. In the meantime, we're encouraged to practice those abilities on quick exchanges of half held beliefs and ideas. That's how I see debates. When we shoot the shit and get in to back and forths about trivial items, they are exactly that, trivial. But the process is important and it allows us to develop the abilities we need to apply ourselves to this world beyond the state we were in when we entered it. It's not religion, it's not buying some other viewpoint at face value, it's creating our own worldviews that shape every miniscule detail of our existence. If somehow that comes about out of some dumb debate, possibly concerning the exact birth year of a minor league athlete or the number of letter Ss there are in Mississippi, I cannot argue with the process. We're a generation of deep thinking, deliberative people, and that should never be mistaken for indifference, even if it results in irreverence.'"

Thirteen

Just type away, any old word will do. It's perfectly natural to get stuck at a certain point.

-Are you frustrated now?

Thank you for your concern, Jonathan, but I'm fine.

-You don't seem fine.

No, really, I'm okay.

-Having trouble creating a story?

You don't give me a lot to work with. You are a flawed individual with less than heroic characteristics. At every chance to improve yourself and your life you've taken half measures or steps backwards. If this was an inspirational, how to book I think the only thing you might have inspired anyone to do was to not be you. This is Jonathan, don't emulate.

-But I'm just a character on a blank page. You are the asshole who created me.

It's always the same with you protagonists. You are placed in the middle of everything. Every scene revolves around your life. If anything happens to you in any of those scenes, it's supposed to be accepted as having great importance and meaning and significance to you. To you! Somehow all of this is about you. Don't give me any attitude that this is my entire fault. Please, I beg you. You! Don't give me any attitude. This entire world, this blank creation, it was empty, and there was nothing, until I created you. I created everything around you for you, and you don't stop to think that perhaps it's all there for you, and you, yes you, are at fault for not making the most of it.

-You want to place guilt on me now?

It's not a guilt trip, Jonathan. I can't make you feel guilty. I'm just the guy who gave you a bit of an outlined sketch, a few things here and there so that everyone would recognise you. You filled in the rest on your own. Guilt, disappointment, underachievement, those are just words. I only write words. You are the one who puts any meaning around them. Don't criticise me for what you've done. I put you in a cubicle. I put you in a bar. I put you in your apartment. That's it, man. Everything you've done in those places has been you. You've carried out the motions without any real intervention. You went in the directions that you led yourself.

-But you are the author.

Yes, I'm. I will take responsibility for starting all this. But you finish it. You are not the character I sketched out in my notebook way back before this. That's not you. That was just a sketch. As soon as that sketch made its way in to being you, Jonathan, it gained character and I can't stop it, you, from being that character.

-I don't like me as a character.

No, you should not. You had a lot more potential in that sketchbook.

-You want me to change?

I already told you I'm not going to do anything ham-fisted to fix you.

-So, it's up to me then, is it?

It always has been. You are the protagonist. This story is all about you.

-That's a lot of weight to carry.

But you don't weigh anything, Jonathan. You are just made up of words, like everything else in this book.

-You make it sound so insignificant.

It's absolutely meaningless.

Fourteen

Jonathan stood waiting for the bus he needed to catch to get to work. He was running a bit late this morning and was worried that he had missed the last wave. It might be another ten or fifteen minutes before the next rush of buses came. Standing on the street next to him were the same characters he always saw in the morning. It seemed when he was running late they were running late, when he was on time they were on time. The odd occasion he was early, sure enough he'd recognise at least a few faces. There was the really cute redhead who never made eye contact. Jonathan didn't know why she never made eye contact with him. Perhaps she was shy. Perhaps she was a snob.

-I don't think she's a lesbian.

Much better, Jonathan.

-If she is, that's not the reason she does not make eye contact. Lots of lesbians will make eye contact with a man. We mustn't generalise.

You really are beginning to evolve.

-Thanks. I didn't think those things before with any seriousness. Usually it was said with irony or some facetiousness.

Well, you have a crappy way of showing it, sometimes.

-Hey, now, I will have you know…wait, I see what you did.

Yep.

Also waiting at the bus stop on a daily basis was an older gentleman who carried a walking stick. Jonathan didn't have too many thoughts on him.

-He walked in to me once.

Oh, right, fine, I will mention that. One time, when Jonathan was about to board the bus, the man with the walking stick pushed himself past Jonathan and hit him in the leg with the end of his stick. Aside from that, Jonathan didn't have too many thoughts about the man with the walking stick.

On the bus, after a few more stops, there were always the same passengers. Jonathan enjoyed observing each of them and trying to note particular characteristics about them. There was one man Jonathan thought looked like an engineer in his early fifties, the kind of fellow who was just going through the motions until retirement. Jonathan always tried to see what books the engineer was reading. It was usually horrible pulp. Some of the man's favourites included Star Wars novels and other light science fiction fare. It wouldn't have surprised Jonathan to learn that the man attended comic book conventions or Jedi training courses. He looked like the kind of man who had come to realise that his daily life was just one long Dilbert strip and in an effort to rejuvenate himself had gotten back in to what he enjoyed in his university days. Jonathan could appreciate the man's fantasies, but didn't like how close to his own reality they struck. Then there was the hipster doofus masquerading as a young professional. He wore ties, but Jonathan thought, just by looking at them, that those ties were worn with the greatest amount of irony possible. This guy looked like one of those people who was a consummate professional at work, who always said the right thing, met his deadlines, and was the first in line to cut up and distribute the cake on a co-workers birthday. But, man, he was only doing it as a joke. Thirty five years later on his retirement, he'll get the gold watch and smile and say thanks, and look sad, then retreat to his dream house and live out the rest of his days, but only ironically. He also liked to wear Ray-Bans. There was the young girl who seemed to, no matter what the weather forecast was, wear a thin, low cut top. Jonathan wouldn't feel so bad about the situation, but he couldn't quite estimate her age. She had one of those faces that she could be anywhere from thirty-five to thirteen. Erring on the side of caution, Jonathan only took a quick peek when it didn't involve straining his neck. There was also a woman that Jonathan recognised from his office building and saw on a daily basis walking down the corridors. He was not sure if they had met before, but he always felt awkward when he saw her and kept his eyes from making contact with hers.

-I'm not a lesbian, either.

Funny guy, Jonathan, you are a funny guy.

It seemed no matter when he took the bus, Jonathan recognised faces. Sometimes it was someone he could pinpoint exactly, like the hipster professional, and other times it was that vaguely familiar face. The kind of person that if you didn't know any better you would think they were the same film extras used in every scene, only wearing different clothes, and maybe a slightly different nose. Jonathan thought the word was filled with people like that. If this world was really all created for his purpose, these people were no more significant than props for another scene.

-I'm not that self-centred, am I?

You are, but that's okay, Jonathan. I think that most people have those thoughts whether they want to admit it or not. It's a dangerous thing to do, to leave them devoid of any meaning. That's partially why we meet them, we put a name to their face, and we make them real to us. Once we do that it makes it harder to hurt them. It makes it harder to be selfish. We can try to walk away, but once we've given meaning, it's nearly impossible to strip away.

-That's why it hurts.

Yeah, it does. That's why no matter how hard we try to say that we've moved on from past relationships; it's never really going to be over. Scars remain. Something that meant a great deal to us at one point can never truly mean nothing, the absence of anything, later. That's just too hard for us to process. Instead we get these scars, even if we know that it's better to move on.

-Like with Eliza.

And every other girl that haunts you, Jonathan.

-Do they feel the same way?

Don't let this inflate your ego any, but yes. Every person on the planet carries the weight of the past.

-I thought you said this was just a story, made up of words.

It is, but you've given those words meaning and you can't ever take that away.

The Dream House

Jon sat at the internet café computer terminal and tried to type away the email as quickly as possible, knowing that his time was running low. He didn't have any more change and didn't feel like having to go break another bill just to get a few minutes more. His whole trip had been like that. Rushing from town to town, taking lots of pictures, stopping to make sure he sent off a postcard from every town, and sending the flirtatious emails back and forth with Veronica. Their time together had come and gone, but Jon found himself pulled back in by cryptic messages. "It would be so great to see you when you get back. I think that I'm able to drive in to see you that weekend." Jonathan was stopping in his university town before he went back to his hometown for the summer. He would be there for almost a week and Veronica was promising to drive down for the weekend. What else could it mean, but that their fleeting moments in time were drawing short so that every one mattered much more than the last and the next would only be so much more special. Jonathan worked himself in to a mental lather as he contemplated the possibilities. There surely was something between Veronica and him; Jonathan knew it. Sparks began to fly whenever he saw her. There just never seemed to be an end to that old flame. It was a dangerous game to play because Jon knew that he was always setting himself up for expectations that may never come to pass. There might always be disappointment. Jonathan thought that things could never be over until they were over. He had heard that in "Love in the Time of Cholera", Marquez has his protagonist sleep with as many women as possible until the time comes when he can be with his true love. The pain would never disappear, but with each conquest the protagonist would feel slightly better, if only for a little while. Jonathan was hoping it wouldn't come to that. He alternated in his mind about whether Veronica was his true love that he was meant to wait for all eternity for, or whether she really belonged in the past and that another, truer true love was out there for him. The most haunting thought that crossed his mind was the possibility that there was no such thing as a true love, pre-destined for each of us. Or, in actuality, the most haunting thought that crossed his mind was the possibility that there was no such thing as a true love, pre-destined for Jonathan. What if the entire world was meant to find that other person that they could call their soulmate and Jonathan was meant to wander the planet lonely for the rest of his existence? Sitting in the empty Berlin internet café made it seem more than possible that the darkest option was the one that would lead Jonathan for the rest of his days.

At the same time, there was an email in front of him that laid open the door to that place Jonathan's mind could most comfortably go. In his mind, the easiest place for happiness was something Jonathan could imagine without much difficulty. It was a place filled with images, mostly some scattered from his past and made to look like a possible future. When he thought of a dream house, it was a combination of the childhood homes he had grown up in, memories of lottery dream homes his family had made him walk through, and real estate photos he had seen in magazines and on websites. Sometimes when he couldn't fall asleep, Jon would try to construct his dream house in his mind. He was past counting sheep. Jon would start with the basement and build from the foundation up, even in a dream. He would think of the dream basement that he wanted. It would have a bar in the back, with a pool table, and the walls would be green or dark blue, something that gives a classic English pub style look to his cave. There would be an entertainment system setup. Jon imagined a big television, the latest and greatest home audio and video, whatever that would be then. No matter how far he thought off in to the future, his imagination for the technology in his dream house looked a lot like whatever the current latest and greatest home audio and video systems looked like. He was a romantic sentimentalist and not a technological futurist. He couldn't predict what things were going to look like, so in his dreams, the pleasant future looked like an idealised version of the past. He would have nice leather couches that also looked a lot like the ones Jon had seen walking past furniture stores. The future he thought of was not about space pods or hover sofas, it was about a domestic life that he wanted a great deal. In the basement there would be a guest bedroom and an ensuite bathroom. Jon didn't want to say so at his young age, but there would have to be a place for his parents to stay when they visited for extended periods. Three days would be nice, but Jon knew at some point they would be old and would need to stay longer. Journeys start taking a toll the more you take and the farther the destination. Jon's journey was already beginning to feel heavy and he was twenty-one. Jonathan would build the rest of his home, the longer he stayed awake, and the more detail he would give. The main level would be finished in the craftsmen style. Jonathan imagined neutral wall colours and basic white doorframes and moulds. It would have some of the modern touches that Jon liked, but still feel warm and welcoming to visitors, keeping a bit of country cottage.

Hard lines and cold materials were the traits of modernism and Jon liked some of the simplicity and minimalism that came with that, but too much just seemed to reinforce his bleak loneliness. Jon would welcome the feminine touches of his future wife, but for now, in his own mind, the dream house was just filled with his own ideas of what a softer touch to décor might look like. He would think of things that in his mind he knew were not the exact things that he must have in a dream home, but they were placeholders for the imagined things that he thought somewhere out there his future wife was awake at night trying to get herself to fall asleep with. Could it be possible?

Jonathan wondered whether Veronica had these same thoughts. It was hard to predict what a woman's imagined dream home looked like. Veronica's apartment had been very bohemian bourgeois, if that description made any sense. She had moved in to a one-bedroom apartment in the university town and made it in to something truly unique for her. The walls were covered with vibrantly coloured paints. Her bedroom was a bright green, splashed across the wall, and drying with varied thickness, some patches revealing spots where either the wall disagreed with the choice of colour, or perhaps not enough primer was used. The tiny living room was a dark burgundy, and filled with one long cloth covered sofa. It was a cosy apartment, the kind of place you could imagine a couple art students sitting around in, discussing the finer points of Marlowe, Malraux, and More, while drinking seven dollar bottles of uncategorised red wine. Jonathan remembered coming over and being drawn in to the warmth of the apartment, that feeling subsidised by Veronica's homemade pâté chinois. The way she made it evoked thoughts of black and white photographs and long flowing dresses. Sitting in the sunny yellow kitchen, eating a slice of shepherd's pie, Jonathan would look around and wonder if this was it. It could have been, Jon thought, it could have been, if it hadn't have been for both of us. That's the silly, ridiculous thing about relationships. We want to believe that it's because the person we're with is not meant for us that things fail. It's harder to imagine that perhaps we aren't meant for ourself. The most destructive force in Jon's life was Jon. He knew it. He suspected that every disappointment along the way also knew it. They probably thought if only this guy could get himself together he'd finally be something decent. Jonathan was certain that he was decent, and that was his first flaw.

Jonathan sat in the internet café and typed as quickly as he could with the foreign keyboard. Letters were hard to predict where they would be. Jon wanted his stupid, inefficient, and familiar QWERTY. He was excited with the possibility that Veronica would meet with him once he returned to Canada. There was an eagerness he read in her words that Jon hoped meant as much as he thought they did.

In the upstairs of his dream home, when he couldn't fall asleep, Jonathan would imagine three bedrooms, two bathrooms (one an ensuite), and a reading room/office. He thought that whomever he would end up with in the future would appreciate having their own personal library and a space to read without distraction. He knew he would. Jonathan thought of Veronica and her boho books, found for a dime at a garage sale, resting on shelves with many of the brand new hardcovers Jonathan bought. It would be an expansive and eclectic collection, theirs, and Jon dreamt of waking up in the middle of the night and walking down the hall from his bedroom to the library. A wingback chair and a thick anthology of short stories would meet his insomnia. Jonathan imagined waking up covered by a blanket, left there by Veronica. Those were his dreams.

Fifteen

Ending a story is actually one of the hardest things to do. You plan ahead, when you start writing, by creating an outline, with some key markers along the way. You know that you need to hit those markers to reach the end you have in mind. In between the markers you allow space for the story to grow organically. Sometimes this organic growth actually causes the writer to miss a key marker or two. Sometimes it shifts the direction a bit off course, but still ultimately leads to the ending that the author intended all along. Other times the natural growth that occurs within the story fundamentally shakes the whole concept the author intended. Key markers get blown to the wayside. The ending becomes unclear. It's a hazy fraction of an idea, ducking beyond the horizon. The author becomes afraid of what it actually might be, not knowing in full, waiting to be led there by the story's progression.

Jonathan was struggling mightily to round out his novel. He had wanted to write about the fun antics that he and his friends experienced in university. He had wanted to write a simple comedy that people could relate to and enjoy. He was not enjoying it. He could relate far too much. The problem with writing about past experiences, Jonathan was discovering, is that inevitably it also digs up old memories, positive and not so positive. Poor decisions and regrettable moments come to light and a new understanding by the author of those events happens. Jonathan didn't look back on these stories as just silly vignettes, as he had intended at the beginning. He was now writing about past happenings that carried current weight. For all of his positing that adult life had made him miserable, Jonathan realised that he had long been experiencing misery.

Jon looked around the bar and saw so few familiar faces. The crowd that was on campus during summer was an entirely different bunch than in the fall. Who were these strangers? Where was Veronica?

In the corner of the bar, Jon saw a small circle of people that he had known as acquaintances. They were at the bar prematurely celebrating their graduation the next afternoon.

"Hey Jon!"

"Oh, hey, how's it going?"

"Awesome! Are you here for the convocation tomorrow?"

"I don't know. I'm going to be in town for a short bit and then I got to head back home for work."

"Right on. What kind of work?"

"Off to a summer camp."

"That should be fun."

"Yeah, it should be. I have wanted to work at one for a full summer for a long time. Finally getting around to doing it before it's too late."

"Definitely! I worked at one three summers ago. Best summer of my life!"

"Wow, great to hear. I hope that works out for me too."

"I'm sure you will have an awesome time."

"Yeah, I hope so."

"Is next year your last?"

"Yeah."

"Well, don't rush through it too fast."

"You going to miss it here?"

"For sure. I have had an amazing time here. This town is crazy. It seems like something was always going on. There was always another adventure waiting."

"What's next?"

"I got a job. I'm starting in August. It's entry level at a big company. Nothing much to begin with, but I will make fifty thousand to start and full benefits."

"That does not sound too bad. I'd love to have a little money. I think it's cost me fifty thousand for this education."

"Probably all worth it though, right?"

"Yeah, probably."

"Well, I'm getting dragged onto the dance floor with my friends now, but if I don't see you before I head out of town, have a good one, and keep in touch."

"Will do. Congrats again on graduating."

"Thanks Jon. Take care of yourself."

Jonathan stood off to the side and drank his beer. Across the bar he saw Veronica. She was looking around in all directions. It was as he had hoped; she was looking for him. Jon's heart skipped a beat and then began to pound irregularly. There was that childish excitement, those butterflies that dance in the stomach. Veronica's perfect face lit up in front of Jonathan. She came close and gave him the biggest hug he had ever felt. There was an extra warmness as her breasts pressed against his chest, thin layers of clothing all that laid between them.

"Hey! You are back!"

"Yeah. How are you?"

"I'm doing great."

"That's awesome."

"How was your exchange?"

"It was great."

"Yeah?"

"Yeah, I loved it."

"Is it weird being back?"

"A little. When I landed at the airport my ears were overwhelmed with the Canadian accents. I had grown accustomed to various English accents. It was weird. I think I grew pretty good at being able to pick them out. Then I landed at the airport here and I was starting to pick out different Canadian accents. I was going, hey I think that guy is from Saskatchewan and those women are from southern Ontario and that couple are Anglo Montrealers. The Newfs were easy."

"Haha, a new talent?"

"Maybe."

"You've already got a few, so this could be a good one to add to your repertoire."

"Gotta have a handy tool box."

"Definitely."

"What are you up to this summer?"

"Just working at an office. Nothing too exciting, you?"

"Going to work at a summer camp."

"Oh, that should be a lot of fun. You would make a great counsellor."

"Thanks. I hope it all works out."

"It should."

"I'm really glad to see you, Veronica. I really am. I'm glad you could make it down this weekend."

"Yeah, well, I knew I had to see you. That's why I told Eric we had to drive down this weekend."

"Eric?"

"Yeah, my boyfriend. We're living together. He thought it would be a good road trip to come down and see some of his graduating friends."

There are certain moments when time almost stops, and everything slows down to emphasise the severity or importance of the situation. People who escape near death accidents swear that they can recall time slowing down and their entire life passing before their eyes. Jonathan experienced his entire life with Veronica pass by his eyes at that moment. He remembered the wine and cheese party where they meant. The first time at the bar when he charmed her with witty banter, egged on by her friends. The party when they were not officially a couple but they stood back to back in different conversation circles and let their hands meet. The discreet way that they both exited the party separately. The end. The first night they lay in bed together and her body fit perfectly next to his. The day he found out an acquaintance of his had passed away. The night they slept together for the first time. The end. The time he looked across the street and saw her leaving her apartment hand in hand with another man. The end. The cold stares as they passed each other on campus. The end. The reconciliation, when against all hurt feelings it was decided that they were better off talking to each other. The end. The misread emails. Today. The end.

"Oh, cool."

"Did I tell you I had a boyfriend?"

"No, I don't think you did."

"So what was your favourite place to visit?"

"Um, probably Spain. Barcelona was amazing."

"That's great. I have always wanted to go. I hear that it's beautiful."

"It is. You can go all the way up this mountain in the city, Mont Juïc, and just look out over everything. From there you can see the Mediterranean on one side and then all the urban sprawl the other. In the middle, in downtown Barca, you can see all the wonderful buildings. The palace, the Olympic buildings, and above them all, la Sagrada Familia."

"What's that?"

"It's the most perfect place. It's an unfinished cathedral designed by Gaudi. When it's all over and complete people will easily recognise it as one of the great wonders of the world. It's so complex and beautiful."

"But unfinished."

"Yeah, beautifully unfinished."

"It sounds really interesting."

"It is. They say that the entire thing is being built by donation. Every brick has been paid for, almost individually."

"Doesn't seem the most efficient way to do things."

"No, probably not. But I guess they're just doing what they can with what they have."

"Do they know when they expect to finish?"

"No, I don't think so. It's hard to say."

"It's hard to predict when things like that finish."

"Yeah, they have their own story."

"It could take forever."

"It could."

"Anyways, I see that Eric is waving me over to him. I should get back. We will talk later, okay?"

"Later."

Sixteen

-Jon?

-Hey Eliza, how's it going?

-Pretty good. I was wondering if you wanted to go for coffee this week.

The ritual had to continue. Jonathan was not sure if he was really in the mood for it again. It was always the same thing. Everything had been done before. The ending never changed, either.

-What day were you thinking?

-Does Thursday work for you?

-I can't do Thursday; I have got soccer that night.

-Oh, alright. What day are you free?

-Are you free a week from Wednesday?

Eliza paused before answering.

-I'm not sure. I will have to check.

-Okay, well let's play it by ear. How about you email me if you are free that night and then we can figure out a time?

-Alright, I can do that.

-Cheers. Talk to you later.

-Bye Jon.

-Bye Eliza.

Jonathan knew that they wouldn't meet for coffee one week from Wednesday. He was not really in the mood and Eliza may have picked up on that. She might also have her own fatigue issues in meeting with him. Say what he might about her repetitive conversations surrounding her boyfriend(s), Jonathan had recently got in to the rut of repetitively talking about his disappointment and dissatisfaction with his career. Eliza and every other friend Jonathan spoke honestly with had been subject to the same things, time and again. Remember, sometimes half the problem is yourself. Jonathan's disappointment came from his own expectations. He wanted everything and he wanted it all now. Patience was a virtue that the majority of the world had in spades in comparison.

-I'm trying.

It takes a while doesn't it?

-It really does.

Jonathan remembered a discussion he had with a mentor like figure a few years before.

-Jon, you've got an expansive, amazingly brilliant mind.

-Thank you. I don't know if I would say that.

-You do. I can tell. We were just talking right now and you started mentioning a seemingly unrelated thing. Your brain is operating at a very high level. You can draw those connections. But the thing I want to ask you, straight up, is what do you want?

-I don't know exactly.

-Exactly. You could be particularly brilliant in any field or interest you apply yourself in.

-This is a pretty good job of filling up my ego.

-I'm not doing that. The thing is with you, Jonathan, is that while you are absolutely filled with the greatest potential I can see that you are your own greatest roadblock. What do you want? You can't have and do everything all at once. Make some priorities. Set goals for yourself. Go and achieve.

It was still the case, Jonathan realised. He wanted to write a fun book about all the wild crazy university antics. He wanted to write a comedy, but every time he tried, his mind drew those seemingly unrelated connections. He wanted a partner to share his life with. Jens Lekman played on the stereo. Ray LaMontagne played on the stereo. Damien Rice played on the stereo. Glen Hansard played on the stereo. The songs just kept playing. Jonathan couldn't let his mind completely disappear and it was driving him crazy. It was killing him from the inside. It was not cancer, but it might as well have been. Jonathan was twenty-five and dying alone.

The List

Charlie was doing push ups on his bedroom floor when Jon came in.

"Hey."

"Hey Jon, just give me a sec."

"Sure."

Charlie finished his set while Jonathan sat down on the end of Charlie's weight bench. Nick's old room felt strange without him. Instead, Jon was meeting with his replacement, both as a housemate, and as the closest thing to a confidant. The midnight meetings had continued in Nick's absence, but had carried an altogether different air. Charlie had pushed himself past just talking about philosophy to actually adopting a way of life. He was trying his damnedest to emulate Nietzsche. If anyone was to become a superman it would be Charlie, the guy who ate cans of tuna with a fork for dinner.

"You gotta be disciplined."

Charlie had nearly been a professional athlete straight out of high school, but instead walked away with the intention of getting a proper education. He set goals and he set limits. He kept both. Jonathan, who would readily admit to being a bit flighty on occasion, immensely respected the discipline that Charlie had. He had come from the same privileged background as their roommate Drew, the man who was given everything with a shrug. Instead of taking handouts, Charlie put himself to work. He drove his own truck, which he saved up for and paid in full. He came from a line of men who believed that if you can't afford to buy something today, you probably don't need it today. Jonathan came from a line of men who believed that if you can't afford to buy something today, you can get it on credit because you might be able to afford it tomorrow, though you still probably don't need it today. Jonathan was not a fool, though Charlie might have thought so.

"Hey, remember when you told me about the list?"

"Yeah, dude."

"I was thinking about doing something like that."

"Cool, man. You totally should. It's good to set goals."

"Do you mind explaining the idea to me again?"

Charlie smiled his half smile and began.

"Back in high school, it was probably eleventh grade, I was told about the idea that you create a list of personal goals. Some could be really short-term things. Some could be things you want to do in the next fifty years. Doesn't really matter. Anyways, you sit down and write the list. You keep it on you, and in your mind you are always, in some way, subconsciously thinking about those goals. Periodically, say every six months, you sit down and re-evaluate. Goals that have been accomplished get crossed off. Goals that

119

you no longer want to do get erased. New goals that you want to do get added. Then you put the list away again and re-evaluate six months from then. You keep doing this until everything on your original list is gone, though the list will have grown and will continue to grow. But, by then you will have accomplished far more than if you just sat around saying I wish."

"I like the idea, man."

"Cool, so you going to try that?"

"Yeah, I'm going to go write the thing now and then put it in my wallet."

"Good place not to lose it."

"Exactly."

Jonathan sat at his computer and realised as he typed this story that his original list was in his wallet. He opened his wallet and saw the small bulge sitting within a pocket. The folded looseleaf paper sat there taunting him almost as much as his credit cards. He unfolded the sheet and looked at the unattended list. He hadn't done a periodic review ever. Not once every six months, not once a year, not ever. Almost four years after writing the list Jonathan hadn't looked at it with any real intent. He had mentioned it to a couple people, who had liked Charlie's idea. But other than that, Jonathan hadn't seriously contemplated the list. It was not burning in to his sub consciousness the way that he knew Charlie's list, fuelled by Nietzsche, was burning in to his. Jonathan looked at the list.

1. Write a novel.

Despite the lukewarm reception to his first book, Jonathan was pleased that he could cross off at least one thing as accomplished. The list had no space for grading, just a simple evaluation for completion.

2. Canoe trip in Yukon.

Jonathan was not too sure whether that was really a goal that needed to be done. It sounded cool so he felt comfortable leaving it on the list. Life is a long time. Maybe one day, or more likely one month, Jonathan would canoe in the Yukon Territory.

3. Live in the woods, off the woods.

Between this and the canoe trip, Jonathan wondered what sort of machismo discussion had spurred the list. Jonathan was looking for life accomplishments, but doubted that he needed to go and prove himself in nature. He liked camping a couple times a year. That was more his pace. Still, he couldn't bring himself to erasing it. His mentor had been right; decision was tough.

4. Get an MA.

Done.

5. Get a PhD.

Maybe? Jonathan was kind of fatigued from all of his formal education as it were. He couldn't rule that out, though.

6. Learn guitar.

Jonathan was slowly working at learning the acoustic guitar. He knew Am, C, D, E, and G chords. He was aware of F, though it was f-ing difficult for him to try.

7. Learn French.

Jonathan a commencé un cours français chaque mercredi après midi. Il a appris beaucoup.

-Oui, c'est ça.

8. Learn Italian.

9. Learn German.

10. Learn Swedish.

None of these things were going to happen anytime soon. Jonathan felt comfortable erasing them. If ever he wanted to begin learning one of them, perhaps once he had mastered his ability in French and Spanish, then he could always add them back to the list.

11. Read Joyce's complete works.

Jonathan's favourite book was *Dubliners*. *A Portrait of the Artist as a Young Man* was the bane of his existence. Ignoring minor works, Jonathan knew he was halfway there with his favourite/least favourite author ever. Ulysses sat on his bookshelf with ominous weight.

12. Read Dostoevsky's complete works.

13. Read Tolstoy's complete works.

It was bound to happen, Jonathan felt. *Crime and Punishment* was fantastic. The Russians would get their due.

14. Travel through Latin America.

15. Travel through New Zealand/Australia/Fiji.

Those two ideas were still very much alive in Jonathan's mind. Along with every other corner of the planet, including places he'd been three or four times.

16. Surf.

17. *Wakeboard.*

Working at a summer camp had made Jonathan realise how terrible he was at water sports. However, in the end, much like skiing and snowboarding, Jonathan's daily life hadn't been too impacted by their absence.

18. *Cross-country road trip in Winnebago.*

Absolutely must still be done.

19. *Start my own business.*

Jonathan had no shortage of ideas and schemes sitting in notepads. This one might still happen at some point.

20. *Paint.*

Done. Poorly, but done nonetheless.

Looking at his list, Jonathan could actually cross off a few items as fully accomplished. He had written a novel, received his Master of Arts degree, and painted. He felt that he could cross off learning guitar and French as in the process of accomplishing, though there may never be a point when he could definitively say he was done with them. The one time he got up on a wakeboard for seventeen seconds was also good enough to cross off. There were some things that he thought he might do without any issue, such as read Joyce, Dostoevsky and Tolstoy. He would also likely travel to the South Pacific and Latin America over the course of his life. He felt pretty confident about that. Same with a cross-country recreational vehicle road trip (he was not tied to it being a brand name Winnebago). After that, everything else were just what ifs, that at the end of it all, didn't matter too much to Jonathan if he never accomplished them. Those aren't really goals, are they?

The one thing that was missing Jonathan spotted right away. It was the most important thing to him and somehow he had failed to place it on the list, let alone at the very top. Pulling out a pen, Jonathan began his new list.

1. *Find the one.*

That was it. To Jonathan nothing else was as important as finding that amazing person that he would want to spend the rest of his life with. There was no point to learning guitar if he couldn't play his wife's favourite song. There was no point to learning French if he had no one to say "Je t'aime" to. Who would want to travel the world alone?

Seventeen

Jonathan woke with a purpose the morning after revisiting his list. There was a new positive energy surging through his body. Possibility was an endless force that stood in front of his every direction.

-I feel good.

Yes, that's what I was saying.

-Cool, keep it up.

You too, Jonathan, you too.

There was something about our protagonist that was instantly more likeable. He smiled. It had been a rare image to see, but it was an infectious smile. When Jonathan showed his pearly whites walking done the street every stranger he passed also smiled back. It was hard to deny Jonathan's earlier suspicions that the world revolved around him when his very own smile could light up the world around him.

-This feels good.

It should. It's a great, fresh start for you. But remember, you've done this before. It's all been done before.

-That's true.

Try not to get stuck in those downward ruts for too long. Those too can bring everyone else down with you.

-Really?

Yes, Jonathan. You've got fabulous powers that you need to be in control of.

-I do?

You are human. Everything about you is powerful, to yourself and others. Be careful what you do with your words, emotions and actions. They can ripple on forever.

-They leave scars.

I'm glad you listen, Jonathan. It seems like you forget too.

-I will try my best not to.

It's okay, it's all been done before and it'll probably all happen again. You can try to learn from your mistakes, but there will always be something new.

Jonathan walked in to the bookstore and went to the biography section to peruse the discounted table. He saw stacks of books of the greatest and most interesting characters of history. Each and every one of them was flawed.

-It takes away some of the mystique, does not it?

Sometimes.

-Sometimes?

Sure, look around and listen.

Two men were standing across the table from Jonathan. In one man's hand was a book about George Washington.

-One of the best military leaders of all time.

-Yeah, probably.

-Right up there with Napoleon and Hannibal, I reckon.

-You think he's that good?

-He defeated the British when they were overwhelmingly the world's greatest power.

-Yeah, I suppose.

-And when most Americans still considered themselves overwhelmingly British. They didn't want a new country. They wanted representation.

-Or fewer taxes.

-That too. That never seems to go away.

-Can't blame them. It's human nature to want to keep what we earn.

-Ha! For sure, could you imagine when fire was invented?

-Um, Og, we really appreciate what you've done and all, with the fire and everything, but we're going to have to take half of it from you.

-Og make fire, Og want all fire!

-Yeah, the thing is Og, that the rest of the tribe is actually without fire and it would be for the best for all of us if everyone has a little fire, what with the cooking of food and the scaring away of sabretooth tigers.

-Og make fire, Og want all fire! You want fire, you make fire!

-Og, we've had a vote. You remember voting? We've had a vote and the tribe has decided you have to share your fire with everyone else.

-Og make fire! Og want competitive advantage!

-Og, it's just the way things are. The rest of the tribe really likes barbequed woolly mammoth and we need fire for that.

-Og make fire, Og want keep fire! Og small business owner!

-Haha, that would have been hilarious. I think I'm going to buy this bio of Washington, though.

-Don't you already have a couple?

-Yeah, but I can't seem to get enough. He was a very complex individual.

Jonathan realised that even though Washington had some major flaws, flaws that would be obvious to anyone who had read one, let alone multiple biographies, the legend of him as a military leader and first president of the United States still remained. When Jonathan thought of Washington he thought of the guy who almost singlehandedly caused the Seven Years' War by accident due to a poor working level understanding of French. That hardly seems like a military genius. But perhaps that just added to the complexity that others saw in him. Flaws become complexities. Each and every one of us was flawed.

-Each and every one of us is beautifully flawed.

It was a horrible conceit that Jonathan had carried with him his entire life, that somehow in order to be special someone was not allowed to have a few warts. Some of his best friends could have blind spots in knowledge or opinion, but that didn't take away from their overall intellectual brilliance. Jonathan had to stop selling people short for their flaws. It was a childhood philosophy that needed to be rekindled. Jonathan needed to see the good in everyone, starting firstmost with himself. All the weight of his own expectations had left him with an invisible hunch. He had been slumping along for years, burdened by impossible standards. Having thought deeply about his goals the night before, Jonathan was trying to align that with his own personal shortcomings.

-I want to find that amazing person to spend my life with.

There was a sense of purpose in Jonathan's life now that rather than being sabotaged by disappointment and impatience was now replaced with optimism and the hope that carrying himself with a smile might bring better results. What was the saying about flies and honey, again?

-I want that amazing person to find that I'm the amazing person they want to spend their life with.

At twenty-five years old, Jonathan was finally beginning to get it. He had always been a slow processor. He was not dumb, in fact he was quite intelligent, but that didn't always resonate through his alternating turns at arrogance and depression.

When he returned home that afternoon, Jonathan sat at his computer desk and began to seriously read what he had written earlier. He didn't like the end. So, as writers often do, he began to change it.

Jonathan sat listening to the old gray men and decided that perhaps there was something beyond all this. Perhaps, while he felt bittersweet about having to leave after only four years, he should remember that bitterness passes and the sweet experiences he had will only grow in posterity. He wanted to share that message with Nick and Gio, wherever they were. He wanted to share that message with Drew and Charlie, with one more year before they would be sitting where he was. Most of all, Jonathan wanted to share that message with himself. He didn't want to try holding on to the vapours of the past. They would be impossible to grasp and frustratingly dissipate. He wanted to move forward to accept all the exciting and wondrous adventures that awaited him. It had been fun to play around, but it was time to get serious about living life. He didn't want to be serious, but he wanted a life that others would take seriously. There was a small, but impossibly important difference between the two.

He wanted to take back his eulogy. This was not a funeral at all, he realised. He wanted to give that commencement speech after all. This was a beginning, and not just of the end, but of that journey in between. Jonathan's mind took over and he imagined himself walking down the aisle and up the stairs on to the stage, taking the microphone and lectern from the old gray man. Turning to his graduating class, Jonathan began anew.

"I'm so excited to be here today. I was not before. I don't know why. I woke with trepidation and fear. I thought today was the end. I can be stupid like that. They call this a commencement for a reason. We're beginning to move on in life, starting today. I know it seems strange that after more than twenty years of living we can finally begin to say that we're beginning. It seems like forever we've been preparing for something, that we've been in school in some form or another. We've been learning, getting educated so that we can finally begin. I used to want to be done as soon as possible. I think it was in high school when I just wanted to leave as soon as possible. I wanted to get here; I wanted to come here, to university to begin to live. I was confused; I don't think I really did know what living was about. I did want to drink, but I'm not sure that's what life is about. The Latin name for alcohol is sometimes aqua vitae, or life water. That's what I thought it was, even before I knew the words aqua vitae. I thought that coming here I'd be able to drink in as much life as I could imagine. I did. I think we all did. I know I remember some epic nights of consumption. I'm sorry to the parents in the crowd for mentioning this, but yes, almost every single one of us has vomited due to too much alcohol. I actually vomited several times. Most of them were in the toilet of my shared bathroom, my bog that I shared with a strange dude named Gio. If you think that's bad, you should probably track him down and make sure he hasn't died due to liver

damage. He once drank enough alcohol to take out a small village in one day. He also alternated between going on all out benders and convalescing in his dorm room bed. It was hardly heroic. It was stupid. We heard about the century club and did it several times. Your kids know what I'm talking about. For the uninformed, century club is a drinking game where you drink one hundred shots of beer in one hundred minutes. You might remember it from the news a couple years back. Some kid drank too much, the object of the game, and then tried to walk home in the freezing cold. He passed out in a ditch and they found his dead body the next morning. Yes, we heard about that. No, that story didn't deter us from playing drinking games. We were young and stupid. We thought that this was what life was about. Another reason I came to university and I don't think I'm alone, was for the purpose of getting laid. There are more than a few blushing faces in the crowd. Oh, good, it's nice to see some alumni parents also blushing. They know exactly what I'm talking about. There was this idea that perhaps by coming here, to some small town where I didn't know anybody I could reinvent myself. I thought I could reinvent my morals. It becomes a lot easier to lower our standards when we're in the process of reinventing whatever standards we might have had before. I'm sure at some point in my future I'm going to be like you parents in the audience. I'm going to be here celebrating the fact that my child has put in four or five years of university and come away with a piece of paper that certifies that they met the standards of the academic world. You are going to hope that along the way your son or daughter has also spent four or five years preparing to leave and live a life that meets the moral and ethical standards of the real world. I don't know what to say about that. I'd like to think that we're all going to leave and treat each other with more respect and dignity than we did here, I really do. I'm not sure if it will happen. There will probably be a few people who allowed their moral and ethical compasses to break while they were here. They may end up living lives that are entirely selfish and will hurt most of the people they come in to contact with in the future. Then there are a lot of people who maybe feel like they faltered while they were here. They feel like they let their families and communities down. Perhaps they come from a religious background and feel like they've fallen. These people may have lost themselves in a moral wilderness while here. Many of them might exit and go in to the real world with a renewed vigour for behaving better. They may try to go and live a proper life, whatever they consider that to be, and they will hurt most of the people they come in to contact with in the future. There is a lot of other people in a lot of other states, but the one thing that I'm going to guarantee is that no matter how you leave here today, and with whatever intentions you leave with, you will hurt most the people you come in to contact with in the future. I want to be clear, and that's important to me, clarity. I'm not trying to be pessimistic. This is not to be pessimistic about us or the future, I just want to leave with a bit of advice. Tread gently, wherever you walk. You are going to leave footprints. People are going to get hurt. We're all human. Even some of the most despicable and discouraging people I met in the course of four years here have feelings. They can get hurt, too. Some of my dearest friends have also been hurt. I have hurt them and they have hurt me. No speech will ever be able to take those moments away. What's done, well, it's pretty obvious that it's *done. I can only sit here today and offer an apology and hope that they all offer the same, whether in their words or at the very least in their hearts, I would hope they feel that I mean the same to them as I once did. I know that despite any hard feelings or past mistakes on my or their part, they will always have a place in my life. I hope that it's not only in my past, but that we might meet again some day, and share a beer or two, and laugh about the good times while we let the past melt away in to the dust. We have no need for malice anymore, we have no need for bitterness or built up resentment. We ought to move forward in to this wondrous future, hand in hand, and support each other. It's dangerous out there and we need all the friends we can get. It will be bumpy, but I think that we can at the very least try to watch out for each other. Don't be a jerk and hopefully that positive energy will be shared with others and reciprocated with us. I don't know whether this is all just platitudes and bullshit or whether or not I'm just rambling out of the dear excitement that you are all finally listening to me. Perhaps I'm just delusional. This is a dream, right?"*

Jonathan looked around and confirmed that he was just daydreaming and that he had not actually been speaking to anyone from a lectern. It didn't make his words mean any less, though.

Acknowledgments

It's all been done before, but I'll continue to thank everyone who has supported me throughout the years. My friends and family have been tremendous and I do not know where I would be without them.

I especially want to thank those who inspired this book and everyone who gave the rough drafts a read in the past two years.

www.ingramcontent.com/pod-product-compliance
Lightning Source LLC
Chambersburg PA
CBHW031834170626
46807CB00004B/1450